The
Holy
Drinker

*For Laven,
In memory of many a fine evening
spent around your table*

Neil

A novel of myth and magic

The
Holy
Drinker

A novel of myth and magic

Neil Randall

KNOX ROBINSON
PUBLISHING
London • New York

KNOX ROBINSON
PUBLISHING

34 New House
67-68 Hatton Garden
London, EC1N 8JY
&
244 5th Avenue, Suite 1861
New York, New York 10001

First published in Great Britain in 2014 by Knox Robinson Publishing
First published in the United States in 2014 by Knox Robinson Publishing

ISBN HC 978-1-908483-90-4
ISBN PB 978-1-908483-91-1
Cover art by Tony Moore
Typeset in Electra by Susan Veach
info@susanveach.com

Printed in the United States of America and the United Kingdom.
www.knoxrobinsonpublishing.com

Who started the fight, us lads could never agree. From what I remember, Pilnyak accused young Igor of drinking his vodka, then Babitsky said something 'bout Pilnyak's betrothed, and before we knew what was happening, we were shouting and cursing at each other, with fists flying everywhere, turning over tables, smashing glasses and all sorts.

'I'll shut you two up, once and for all,' cried Pilnyak, waving a broken stool above his head. 'I'll make you sorry you were ever born.'

'For goodness sake,' shouted Petrov, the innkeeper, rushing around the bar. 'Stop it! You're tearing the place apart.'

'What's wrong?' Babitsky shouted at Pilnyak, ignoring Petrov's call for calm. 'Everybody knows that girl of yours spends most of her time on her back.'

Enraged, Pilnyak threw the stool across the room, narrowly missing Babitsky and young Igor. Those not involved in the scuffle dived for cover, while us lads threw flurries of drunken kicks and punches, wrestled each other to the floor, scrunching 'round over broken glass.

'Twas a right good tussle. And 'twasn't 'til Volya-the-Pouch readied to crack a bottle over his brother's head, and a booming voice called out from the depths of the tavern, that everyone, Volya included, stopped and turned round. Seated in the far corner of the room was an old man with a straggly white beard and with bandages wrapped 'round his eyes. Unsteadily, he got to his feet, and with the aid of a wooden cane, shuffled his way forward, barging his way in between the warring siblings.

'Look at yourselves, brothers!' he cried. 'Ashamed, you should be, 'bout to smash each other's heads open on account of that evil spirit you've been pouring down your throats.' He jabbed the cane in Volya's direction. 'Let me tell you a story 'bout the perils of drink, my lads. Let me tell you 'bout old Maximov, once a resident of these here parts.'

'Maximov?' said Volya, lowering the bottle.

'Aye, Maximov the drinker they used to call him. And an apt name 'twas, too, 'cause that heathen's appetites almost destroyed this town and everyone in it.'

1

Chapter One

Even by Maximov's standards, this five-day drinking binge had been excessive. It all started in the village of N. on a freezing cold winter's morning. Having journeyed ten or so versts, Maximov hoped to sell some firewood to Kondratiev, a local landowner. After much haggling, the two wily old men adjourned to Kondratiev's kitchen for a glass of vodka. In those days no transaction was complete until the wheels of commerce had been well and truly oiled.

'Your good health, Anatoly Vasilevich,' said Kondratiev, tossing back his vodka and reaching for the bottle.

Each time he refilled Maximov's glass, the stout, ruddy-cheeked merchant brought it to his lips, breathed the fumes in through his bulbous nose, and quickly swallowed, savouring that pure liquid warmth as it spread through his body. Then he wiped a hand over his moustache, and his dark brooding eyes–just for the flash of a second– cast a greedy glance at the holy bottle.

'Here, Anatoly Vasilevich, have one more glass before you go.'

Maximov's hand was already poised.

'That's very good of you, Ivan Denisovich. Neither your face nor your generosity will I ever forget.'

A few hours later, in high spirits, his pockets jangling with silver rubles, Maximov left Kondratiev's house, clambered onto his cart and turned to his skinny young driver, whose shivering hands could barely grip the reins.

'Best you get a shift on, Peter, my lad. That sky don't look too sharp to me. I reckon we'll be seeing snow long before we get ourselves in sight of home.'

The youngster whipped the two nags until they ambled forward, scrunching their hoofs along the icy lane rutted with potholes.

Maximov buttoned up his sheepskins, put on his cap and wrapped a rough woollen blanket around his shoulders. As the horses broke into a trot, he looked out over the snow-covered fields, took in a great lungful of cold, crisp air, and, when sure Peter was not looking, put a hip-flask to his lips and knocked back a little cherry brandy. He could not help chuckling to himself. The wood sold to Kondratiev, he later boasted, was, at best, of mediocre quality.

It was not long before Peter caught scent of the alcohol, and turned to see Maximov with his mouth around the flask.

'Hey, Anatoly Vasilevich, couldn't I have a drop of that stuff? The cold's seeping right into my bones, it is.'

Maximov whisked the hip-flask back under his blanket.

'Not on your life,' he said. 'Your poor old mother would never forgive me. And besides, you don't want to start drinking–not now, not ever. It's evil stuff, bad for you, it is, ruins your health, pickles your brains, stops you from satisfying the womenfolk.' He puffed out his cheeks. 'Take it from me, someone who knows: drinking is the last thing a good, God-fearing youngster like you wants to do.'

Thick snowflakes started to fall from the darkening sky, settling steadily on the ground, until the banks at the sides of the track seemed to tower above the cart and the road up ahead looked almost impassable.

'Best we head for Glinka's tavern,' said Maximov. 'We don't want to get ourselves caught up in this here storm.'

And there is no better sight to a traveller than a tavern with its chimney smoking, the lights shining from the windows, and the faint smell of roasting meat wafting on the cold evening air.

Before the cart had even come to a stop, the tavern door swung open and out walked Glinka himself. An imposing sight, with not a hair on his head, and wearing a shiny leather apron, he beckoned the new arrivals inside, where voices, laughter, the clatter of pots and pans and a crackling fire sounded so welcoming.

'Come, quickly. It's deathly cold out here, lads.' Glinka took a step closer and squinted up his eyes. 'Why, is that my good friend Anatoly Vasilevich?'

'That it is.' Maximov alighted, pushing the blanket off his shoulders. 'Have you room for a couple of weary travellers?'

Glinka grinned and rubbed his hands together.

'For such a valued patron as you, Anatoly Vasilevich, we'll make space somehow, even if this weather has drawn many a man off the road tonight.' He pointed to a wooden outbuilding. 'Have your boy tether your beasts in there. I'll make sure they're well-provided for, too.'

Maximov turned to Peter.

'You heard him, lad. Get those horses sorted out before you think about putting your feet up.'

The air inside the tavern was heavy with tobacco smoke. On one set of wooden benches sat a few morose-looking travellers, with jugs of wine or vodka on their tables. On another, far more uproarious folk laughed and joked and played a few hands of cards. Two serving girls—one of about seventeen, fair-haired and petite, the other a little older, dark-haired and buxom—provided the refreshments from a bar piled with all sorts of savouries, pies and pickled snacks, to help stimulate a thirsty man's appetite.

Glinka dragged a table and chair over to the roaring fire.

'What can we get you, Anatoly Vasilevich? Vodka?'

'Aye, you know me, old friend—vodka, it is.'

And here his drinking spree started in earnest.

The first jug was dispatched before Peter had returned from the stables—but the youngster would have been none the wiser. For Maximov was the kind of drinker who looked and sounded the same after two drinks as he did after two dozen: irrepressible, garrulous, his face red and his eyes alive.

As he tucked into the second jug, he stripped down to his shirtsleeves, called the serving girls over at every opportunity, patted their behinds, and told them all kinds of unlikely stories. Every now and then he broke off from his drinking to chat with people at nearby tables, enquiring about their business, where they had come from and where they were destined tomorrow. Drink turned the old merchant into a completely different man. If sober, and he saw a crippled peasant woman crawling through the snow, he would not so much as pass her by as trample her underfoot. If drunk, he was known to embrace complete strangers, fling his money around, pledge lifelong allegiance, offering them all his worldly possessions.

With none of his previous stinginess, he bought a round of drinks and ordered Peter some meat broth and a bread roll.

'Take note, my lad,' he said. 'This is how a working man unwinds after a hard day. Without it life wouldn't be worth living.'

Peter bit into his bottom lip and cast a hopeful glance at the fresh jug of vodka on the table.

Spotting this, Maximov moved it well out of arm's reach.

'I said "man" not boy. A couple of glasses of Kvass before bed'll do you, but don't you be getting a taste for anything stronger.'

Maximov proceeded to eat enough to satisfy two or three men— young, hard-working men, at that. He drank another whole jug of vodka to himself, unbuttoned his tunic so it hung loose, revealing his huge, drink-swollen belly. He invited a few like-minded revellers over to his table, told them more jokes and stories, shot to his feet and jigged around on the spot. In his excitement, he spat on the floor, expelled wind in the most base and extravagant ways, wrung his hands, and wiped his brow with a filthy handkerchief.

In this fashion the midnight hour approached.

'Glinka, my dear old friend,' said Maximov, slumped in his chair, his loosened shirt, trousers and scuffed leather boots spattered with food stains. 'What'd you say to a little entertainment, eh? A band? P'haps those gypsies from across the meadow?'

'But it's late, Anatoly Vasilevich, and the weather hasn't let up. The roads are all but impassable and the wolves can be aggressive this time of year.'

Maximov waved the landlord's words away.

'No matter. Send my boy, Peter. He knows the way and'll be only too happy to get himself down there.'

Glinka stood there rubbing his chin, as if deep in thought.

'Tell you what, Anatoly Vasilevich. Why don't I get old Pasha to tune his balalaika? He can sing all right. And if it's not to your taste, I'm sure my serving girls can hum a decent enough tune.'

This more than satisfied Maximov.

'Good idea,' he said, before winking and tapping his nose. 'And don't you worry. I'll make it worth their while. They can have a right good drink on me, they can. I'm celebrating. It's my name-day today.'

'Really?' said Glinka. 'Well, er…many happy returns, Anatoly Vasilevich, all you wish for yourself. And if that's the case, you must try some of my special wine—redder than rubies, it is, fit for the Tsar himself.'

'Fit for the Tsar himself!' Maximov roared with laughter and banged one of his great fists against the tabletop. 'Then bring out a few bottles, Glinka, old pal. Let's drink to good health and a long life.'

As Pasha tuned his balalaika, the other customers dragged their chairs closer, and a respectful silence fell over the tavern. For effect, Glinka blew out the candles and extinguished the lanterns on all but the table nearest to the wiry, straggly-haired musician.

Running his gnarled fingers over the strings, he began to sing in a voice full of melancholy.

'Beyond the hills where the snow lies deep,
The ice-fields crack and the tempests blow,
Where angrily bow the pines and firs
The Cossack's bones lie beneath the snow.'

Maximov stood up. Tears were already rolling down his flushed cheeks.

'As the Cossack lay dying he pleadingly asked
That above him a mound should be piled for his tomb,
And a hazel tree from his native land
Should be planted in brilliant flower to bloom.'

Maximov persuaded Pasha to sing the song countless times over. During each rendition the old merchant shook his head from side to side and wrung his hands in despair not excitement this time. After drying his eyes, he ordered a dozen bottles of Glinka's wine and toasted everyone he could think of toasting, from the Tsar to Kondratiev, the very man he had swindled a handful of hours previous, while proclaiming the wine to be the best he had ever tasted.

'Glinka, you must let me buy two cases to take home with me tomorrow.'

By the time the last of the bottles had been drained, Glinka walked over and shook Maximov's shoulder.

'Time we found you a bed, eh, Anatoly Vasilevich?'

Maximov lifted his head from the tabletop and opened one drink-reddened eye.

'Say, Glinka,' he whispered, beckoning him closer, 'couldn't you send one of your serving girls to lie next to me for an hour or two?'

Glinka's face creased.

'Oh, I don't know about th–'

'Call it a favour between friends,' said Maximov, straightening in his chair. 'I just want to feel a young body next to mine on my name-day–no funny business, I promise you that.'

'Okay, okay,' said Glinka. 'I'll go and wake young Nina.'

True to his word, Glinka provided Maximov with one of the best rooms in the tavern, a snug little space on the ground floor, with a glowing stove in one corner and a stand and wash-basin in the other.

Just after Maximov slumped down on the feather mattress, Nina, the younger and slimmer of the two serving girls, crept into the room. In only a slip of a nightgown, her hair hanging loose over her shoulders, she leaned over Maximov, unsure if he was asleep or not.

'Don't worry, my girl,' he whispered, patting the space beside him. 'Lie yourself down. I won't hurt you. I just want to stretch out here for a while and listen to you breathe.'

Reassured, she laid down next to him.

After a moment or two had passed, he reached out and stroked her hair with a tenderness that put her completely at ease. Rolling onto his side, he huddled closer, pressed his nose against her soft skin, savouring the freshly-soaped scent of her young body.

'Good night, Natashka, sweet dreams, my precious.'

Then he smacked his lips, rolled onto his back and fell into a deep, fathomless, drinker's sleep.

Chapter Two

Light snow fell over the bustling market square. On sale from dozens of stalls were hand-woven rugs and colourful fabrics, handicrafts, suckling pigs, bottled milk and great heaps of freshly-baked bread; the aroma of which wafted on the freezing cold air. Traders haggled and cajoled, offering up their goods, some more forcefully than others. Men and women wrapped in sheepskins trudged through the snow, carrying trays of eggs, squawking chickens and jars of preserves. Children in hats and scarves laughed and chased after each other, and threw the odd snowball at unwitting passers-by. A few peasants knelt by the main thoroughfare, begging for alms. And some speechifying socialist called for further land reforms.

As soon as the children saw Maximov's cart, they ran over and crowded round on either side.

'Maximov kissed his wife goodbye, and then he drained the pitcher dry,' they sang, while skipping through the slushy puddles at the sides of the track. 'Old Maximov's kissed his wife goodbye, and all for a drink of liquor.'

'Get away!' Maximov shouted. 'Get away, I said!'

'He's sold his wife! He's sold his dagger!' the children continued, laughing and clapping, '–swapped 'em for a drink of liquor!' before darting out of sight, when Maximov brandished a fist.

'Ruffians!' he cried, half making as to get to his feet, before turning to Peter. 'I think we'd best stop off at Pogbregnyak's for a drink, my lad, just to put a bit of life back in our legs.'

When the old merchant pushed open the tavern door, a cloud of cheap tobacco smoke drifted out. It was unusually dark inside; the low beams and frosted windows giving the place a dingy, gloomy feel. In one corner by the counter stood Pogbregnyak and the moneylender, Chernov (the closet person Maximov had to a friend). In the other corner sat two jaundiced old men, no more than raggedy bags of skin and bone, with their elbows resting on their tables, staring blankly into space.

'Ah,' said the tall, rangy landlord, squinting up his narrow Kirghiz eyes. 'The traveller returns.' He loped around the counter and took a glass from the top shelf. 'I trust your trip was a success, Anatoly Vasilevich, you wouldn't have been away overnight otherwise. Now, what can I get you? Vodka?'

'Aye,' said Maximov, walking over. 'Vodka it is. Fill a pail. I'm sure we'll find it a good home.'

Chernov, a well-dressed man of fifty, with thinning hair and an ashen face, took his cigarette from his mouth, wafted the smoke away, leaned close and stared hard at Maximov.

'Whatever's happened to your lips, Anatoly Vasilevich? They've turned a very strange colour.'

Maximov rubbed his fingers across his lips and examined the dead skin that detached, blackened by red wine.

'That's a story in itself,' he said, wiping his hand on his trousers. 'On my travels, I happened upon some of the finest wine a man could drink–fit for the Tsar himself, it was.'

Chernov looked intrigued.

'Really?' He tossed his cigarette to the floor. 'And did you happen to bring a sample back with you?'

'As a matter of fact, I did.'

The door swung open. Peter trudged into the tavern, rubbing and blowing on his hands.

Maximov turned his head.

'Peter, go and fetch a couple of bottles of that wine from the back of the cart. And afterwards, best you stay outside to keep an eye on it. There's no end of thieving bandits drawn to town on market-day.'

The boy's face dropped.

'But, Anatoly Vasilevich, it's freezing out th–'

'And be quick about it,' said Maximov, cutting him short.

When Peter had brought the wine inside, Pogbregnyak eased the cork from the first bottle, and with much ceremony, poured it into three glasses.

'It certainly looks like a good vintage,' said Chernov, holding his glass up to the relative light. 'See the way it sloshes around?–full of body–that's a very good sign, so I'm told.'

All three men raised their glasses and took a first sip.

'Cor!' said Pogbregnyak, smacking his lips. 'I could get used to that. You'll be turning us into gentry yet, Anatoly Vasilevich.'

Maximov chuckled.

'And I've got plenty more where that came from,' he said, draining his glass. 'Come on, Pogbregnyak, top us up, and then we'll open another.'

In due course, Maximov told them all about yesterday's adventures, embellishing with each glass of wine. He spoke of outwitting Kondratiev, the reception he received at Glinka's tavern, how many jugs of vodka he drank, and the special attentions bestowed upon him by the buxom young serving girls. On more than one occasion he attempted to sing Pasha's melancholy ballad, confusing the lyrics so badly it turned into nothing more than a bumbled stream of nonsense. He banged his fist on the counter, turned and pivoted, pointing to imaginary friends and foes; he jigged on the spot, and drank to the dregs of the wine, refusing to leave "any tears in the bottle."

By nightfall, he was taking huge mouthfuls of vodka before each glass of wine.

'You're asking for trouble,' said Chernov, his own eyes red and beady through drink, 'mixing things up like that. You know what they say about the grape and the rye.'

Maximov shook his head.

'Nonsense, Vasily Ivanovich,' he said. 'You'll not make yourself bad on this stuff—it's impossible—nectar from the gods, it is.'

For three days and three nights, he stayed at the tavern, only relinquishing his spot at the bar when passing out. With the aid of Chernov, Pogbregnyak dragged the old drinker to a flea-bitten mattress out back, wrapped a blanket around him, and let him sleep it off.

After a few hours, he marched straight back into the tavern, as if he had never been away, picked up his glass and continued drinking.

On the fourth night, full up with wine and vodka, his lips as black as Ukrainian soil, he finally told Peter to drive him home.

His two-storey house, with its numerous outbuildings, was a ramshackle eyesore, but Maximov saw no reason in spending money for appearances sake. If the iron roof leaked or the windows emitted a hellish draught, he was more inclined to put a bucket down to collect the water, and to wrap himself up in an extra blanket at night. In a strange way, he liked the dilapidated porch, broken fence, and yard strewn with all kinds of cast-off materials.

'Come on, Anatoly Vasilevich,' said Peter, nudging Maximov in the ribs. 'We're home now.'

With difficulty, he managed to get his master out of the cart and halfway along the icy path leading to the front door.

'You're a good lad, you are, Peter.' Maximov let go of the boy's arm. 'Shush. Look up there.' He staggered slightly, pointing to a clear night sky alive with twinkling stars. 'Breathe in that air.' He took a deep, wheezing breath. 'That's what it's all about—the big wide world. Yes. If I was your age again, you wouldn't find me wasting my time in a miserable town like this. I'd be off exploring, sailing the seas, mixing with the gentry folk, chasing after women, having a high old time of it, I would.' He took one last, rueful look at the heavens. 'Life's for living. You want to get out of here, my boy, soon as you get a chance.'

Having heard voices, Maximov's housekeeper, Marfa Orlova, unbolted the front door. In a kerchief, shawl and long frayed undershirt, this stooped, prematurely aged woman with a face full of wrinkles, stood there mumbling and cursing under her breath.

'Look at the state of you!' she cried as Maximov angled himself in through the door. 'How am I ever going to get you upstairs?'

Maximov, with that peculiar drinker's gait—part shuffle, part stumble—headed in the direction of the stairs, bumping into wooden pallets stacked with all kinds of junk, knocking over a coat stand and a pile of old newspapers, bashing into a crate full of empties, jangling the bottles inside, while all the time waving away Marfa's concerns.

He started to climb the stairs.

Each wooden step groaned under his weight. He wobbled, tottered, grabbed onto the banister and righted himself before eventually navigating his way to the top.

Bundling his way along the landing, he pushed open a door, fell into his room and collapsed out on the settee, already made up with pillows and a blanket.

In the silent darkness, he rolled onto his side and felt five days worth of strong drink slosh around in his belly, as if a whole case of wine could pour out of his mouth at any moment.

The room started to spin.

His wheezing breaths were rapid and strained now. Every time he shifted position sharp pains shot up his back and his heart pounded against his chest. Far more distracting, though, were the jumbled assortment of memories, some distant, some from the last few days, that were accompanied by a terrible sense of guilt and regret, as if he had done something very wrong, whether years or hours before, that had shamed him to his very core.

He rolled onto his back and stared at the ceiling, where something familiar started to form. The harder he stared, the more vivid and alive the vision became, until he could see himself as a young man again, a strong, brave Cossack, someone prepared to take on the world and everybody in it.

He closed his eyes. He could hear sickles scything through corn, panting breath, and a sweet burst of girlish laughter that sounded precious and comforting to his ears. It was then Maximov's spirit, that of the young man he had once been, got up from the settee and drifted into the dream world on the ceiling, back to a day when he was working in the fields with his family. Under a harsh afternoon sun, the sweat pouring down his bare chest, he drove his own sickle through the corn, and heard that gentle burst of laughter once again. He turned his head and saw a young girl, his former sweetheart, Natalia, staring back at him. He had forgotten how fresh and beautiful she had been then, her chestnut hair falling over her shoulders, her skin white and soft, her eyes jewel-like in her slender, smiling face. He had forgotten what it felt like to be looked at in that way by a woman, too, how proud and vulnerable it made him feel, vulnerable because he did not know the nature of his true feelings yet.

The dream vision deepened.

Now they were walking hand-in-hand through the forest, in the cool dark shadows of overhanging trees, talking in that special way young lovers do, where nothing else in the world matters apart from the time they spend together. A little way along they came to a clearing and sat by the banks of the river, like they used to do every Sunday after church. They did not speak for a while; just being close to each other conveyed more than words ever could. Maximov stretched out and listened to the wind gently rustle through the nearby reeds. He watched the sunlight reflect off Natalia's hair, and the way she wrinkled her nose and pushed strands of it away when the breeze wafted it over her face.

'Natashka, my dearest.' He sat up. 'Come over here.'

She smiled and shuffled along the grass. He took her in his arms, smelt the heady flowery fragrance of both her hair and skin, closed his eyes and kissed her soft lips.

Memories flooded his consciousness, in the same way all that vodka and wine had flooded his body.

He remembered how excitedly they used to talk, about getting married, of starting a family of their own one day. Every moment seemed stolen back then, in lieu of a time when they were old enough to be man and wife.

'Will you still love me when I'm a plump old woman with wrinkles all over my face?'

'Aye, that I will, my darlin', 'cause I would've watched each of those lines trace a path across your skin, so they'd be special to me, just like you'll always be special to me, every bit of you.'

'Special? How can an ugly wrinkle be special?'

"Cause it would be a marker of a moment in our lives together, a moment I loved you best.'

He remembered how sad she looked when he clambered upon his horse and went off a-warring with the rest of the Cossacks. He remembered her love-letters, those he had to get other men in his regiment to read, saying she would wait for him forever, that she would kill herself if he were to die, how her life meant nothing unless he was in it.

Those two years away passed slowly.

Now he recalled the emptiness he felt for the rest of his days, knowing something special had been forever lost, when returning a very different man, marked by his experiences at war, to find Natalia in the arms of his cousin, married and with a child to boot.

'I'm so sorry, Anatoly,' she whispered to him one day. 'I thought you were dead. I would never have…'

He opened his eyes, and with a thump, the tired old man he was today fell out of his dream vision and crashed back down onto the settee.

His face became wet with tears, because that was the moment he truly died, the moment he saw Natalia with another man's baby in her arms, whether his body carried on living or not.

Nothing I hoped and dreamed of when I was younger ever came true, he thought to himself, with a bitterness that choked him all over again. He tried to lift a hand to brush the tears away, but could no longer muster the strength. All he could do was lie there and stare at the ceiling, at Natalia's face, the fading memories of life as it once was and could never be again.

'Old Maximov's kissed his wife goodbye,' he heard those children singing in his head, 'and all for a drink of liquor…'

And he knew then that he had wasted his life, wasted any chance of true happiness, love, a family of his own, on vodka and cheap wine, that he had traded all his good, strong and youthful years for the bottom of a never-ending glass.

And it was then that something very strange happened to Maximov the drinker. All that wine really did start to pour out of his mouth and flow down his chin. And not just a trickle, either, but a great flood of the stuff. Once again, he tried to lift a hand to stem the tide, but it was not just his mouth expelling wine now, but his whole body. It poured out of his eyes, his ears, his nose, until he was no longer skin and bone but liquid, until old Maximov and the settee where he lay had been transformed into a great vat of ruby-red wine.

Chapter Three

Next morning, Marfa Orlova rapped on Maximov's door.

There was no response.

'The drunken old fool,' she muttered under her breath. 'It'll take me all day to wake him now.'

She opened the door and walked inside.

'Anatoly Vasilevich, you must get up, it's nearly…' she trailed off, gasped and brought a hand to her mouth. Where Maximov's settee had previously been was the glowing vat of ruby-red wine.

Marfa grabbed hold of the wall to support herself; such was the potency of the wine's heady alcoholic fumes.

'My God!' She crossed herself, bundled her way down the stairs, pushed open the front door and stumbled out into the snow-laden streets.

'Help!' she cried, almost slipping on the icy path. 'Help! Please!'

Chernov and Captain Levsky, head of the local garrison, happened to be passing.

'Whatever's the matter?' asked Chernov, rushing over. 'Has Anatoly Vasilevich fallen out of bed again?'

'No, that's just it,' she gabbled. 'His bed's up and disappeared, that's what, been replaced by a big tank full of red wine.'

Chernov exchanged a confused glance with the tall handsome officer who had just joined them.

'What are you talking about, woman?' said Levsky, smoothing

18

down his side-whiskers. 'You're all a fluster. You've not been drinking this morning, have you?'

'Drinking?' Marfa flashed him a wild stare. 'I wish I had. Then I wouldn't have seen the devil's work at play. Come inside if you don't believe me. The evil one has spirited the master away.'

Father Semyon came out of a thatched cottage across the street.

On seeing the bearded, diminutive priest, Marfa shouted and waved her hands above her head.

'Oh, Father, thank God. You must come, quickly. Something evil is afoot.'

The startled holy man shuffled over, took Marfa by the hands and asked her to explain exactly what had happened.

'You see, Father,' said Levsky, 'the woman has had some kind of breakdown. Best we get the doctor to her.'

The kindly-faced priest shook his head.

'Let's not get carried away. Let's go inside and see what this is all about, eh?'

When the three men got upstairs they could scarcely believe their eyes.

'Heaven help us,' said Father Semyon, staring into the wine, the ethereal glow casting a curious, red-tinted shadow across his face. 'I don't think I've ever seen the likes of this before.'

Levsky turned to Marfa.

'And the last time you saw Maximov, he was on his way to bed?'

'That's right,' she replied. 'I stood at the bottom of the stairs and heard him slump down on the settee. Not a glimpse have I seen of him since.'

As Father Semyon and Captain Levsky asked Marfa more questions, Chernov sidled over to the wine. With a quick glance over his shoulder, he readied to dip his finger in for a quick taste.

'Don't touch it, you fool!' cried Levsky. 'We don't know what's in there yet. It could be poison.'

Chernov swung round.

'Poison?' he spluttered. 'Don't be so ridiculous. It's wine, and good wine at that, you can tell by the smell of it. And anyway, I can easily explain all this. Anatoly Vasilevich was away on business a few days back. Over the course of his travels he met a wine merchant, who let him have a few cases at a knock-down price. Maximov must've set all this up when he got back.'

Father Semyon shook his head.

'If that's so, then where is Anatoly Vasilevich now? The last time he was seen, he was dead drunk, stumbling up those very stairs.' He pointed to the opened door. 'And his settee, the one Marfa made up not an hour before he returned, has disappeared, too.'

'Come now, Father,' said Chernov. 'This is no more than one of Anatoly Vasilevich's business ventures. He's always looking for a way to make a bit of extra money.'

The priest looked offended.

'It's you who's mistaken, Vasily Ivanovich. For a start, how could he have got such a great vat up that narrow staircase? And look at the wine; it looks unreal, as if invested with mystical powers. No. Marfa is right. This is a miracle of some sort, a sign from above. And before we do anything, we must contact the highest religious authority in the region.'

Even Levsky, a practical man, who usually gave short shrift to any superstitious nonsense, was swayed by Father Semyon's arguments. The facts of the case were such, it was clear something out of the normal grasp of human comprehension had taken place here.

He walked over to Marfa and put his hands on her shoulders.

'You mentioned something about Maximov's driver—a young lad called Peter, didn't you say?' He turned to the other two men. 'Perhaps he can shed some light on the matter. Marfa, go and fetch him, will you? I think it best we talk to him before we make any rash decisions.'

Peter arrived within the quarter-hour.

Like the others, he too was so taken aback by the wondrous sight in Maximov's room, it took a good few minutes before he could answer any of their questions.

'No, the master only bought two cases of wine from Glinka, and him and his friends, including Mr Chernov there'—Peter pointed at him—'saw those off in the tavern over the last few nights.'

'And he didn't mention anything about a delivery of any sort?'

asked Levsky, as if conducting an interrogation. 'He didn't make any arrangements for the receipt of more wine?'

'Not as far as I know,' the boy replied. 'But even if he did, how would he have got that great thing up the stairs? He could barely put one foot in front of the other when I left him. It doesn't make any–'

'All right, Peter, all right,' said Levsky, raising his hands. 'Such things have not escaped our notice.' He started pacing the room. 'Gentlemen, this is what I propose we do. I shall send a telegram to Petersburg this very morning, asking for some advice on how best to proceed. Father Semyon, I suggest you contact your superiors at the Church, informing them of exactly what has taken place here. In the meantime, we best keep this between ourselves.' He stared hard at Chernov. 'No gossiping at the tavern. Understand?' The moneylender nodded his head. 'There's no need to start any wild rumours. If anybody asks, Maximov is still in bed, sleeping off the excesses of the last few days. Agreed?'

He looked at everyone else in turn and they too nodded their heads.

'Right, for now, I'll arrange for some of my men to guard the house until I receive further instructions. Marfa, can I rely on you to keep your front door locked and let no one enter this room, under any circumstances, until they arrive?'

'Of course. I'll barricade it up if I have to.'

'That won't be necessary,' said Levsky. 'But perhaps young Peter would be good enough to keep you company, just in case any unwelcome visitors decide to call round.'

Peter stepped forward and puffed out his chest.

'I'd be more than happy to, sir,' he said, duty-bound to remain at the house until his master returned, or the mystery surrounding his unlikely disappearance had been solved.

'Good,' said Levsky. 'That's settled, then. We'll leave you to lock the room, Marfa.'

The three men, with Peter not far behind, walked out and started to climb down the stairs.

As Marfa was about to close the door, a distinct gurgling noise emanated from the vat. Turning her head, she stared at the beautiful wine glistening so enticingly, as if encouraging her to take a sip. Spying an empty bottle on the window-ledge, she rushed over, grabbed it, filled it with wine, and hid it on the landing.

That evening, she went through her time-served routine: retiring to her room, sliding the lock across the door, lighting a candle, placing a glass on the stand beside the settee she slept on, and pouring out some illicit alcohol. Only tonight it was not the dregs from some locally-distilled vodka or cheap, unpalatable wine that Maximov had left discarded and forgotten around the house, but the bottle she procured from the vat upstairs.

As was her want, she did not guzzle back the wine straight away, but left it on the stand, while she rummaged amongst her possessions for a few old baby clothes, those her own children had never lived long enough to wear. Of the nine babies the unfortunate woman had borne, not one had survived beyond the first few months. Humming a sad tune, she played with a pink bonnet, running her crooked fingers over the woollen material, now and then bringing it close to her nose, breathing in the lost scent of a newborn child.

After a while, she reached out and took a mouthful of wine, savouring the smooth elixir as it slid down her throat, making her feel warm and dreamy inside, closer to a past she could never bear to be parted from. Closing her eyes, she remembered how nice it felt to be pregnant, to know that a little body was growing inside of her. She remembered all the times she felt her sons or daughters kick or shift around in her belly, and how special it made her feel, to know that she was about to become a mother for the first time and have a family of her own, and how she would make sure her children had all the love she could give them, something sadly lacking in her own upbringing.

When she opened her eyes again, she was no longer in her dreary room with its colourless walls anymore, but back inside her old shack, the one just outside of town that she shared with her husband. She looked around. The stove glowed from the back room, chairs stood either side of a wooden table, the ikons on the dresser, the window looked out on the dirt-track leading to the market square, and the settee was covered with baby clothes—everything exactly as she remembered it.

In shock, she tried to stand up, but her swollen tummy prevented her from getting anywhere close to her feet. It was then her apprehension turned to joy—a pure exalted kind of joy—the kind she felt when she first learned she was with child, and she sunk back into her chair and ran her hands over her stomach. It was true: she was pregnant again.

The door swung open.

In walked her husband, a strong, well-built young man, with a big smile on his freckled face, the smile he always wore during those first years of their union, before he took to drink and started to beat and humiliate her.

'Greetings, my darlin'.' He planted a kiss to her forehead. He smelt of sweat, of the fields, the honest and holy scent of hard work. 'Look what I've got for you.'

He pulled a pink baby bonnet out of his tunic pocket.

Marfa's face became wet with tears. The bonnet was so tiny and perfect, each woollen stitch sewn with the utmost care.

The dream vision deepened.

Now Marfa was walking through the market square, holding her husband's arm. He looked so handsome in his best Sunday tunic she could feel the jealous glances of the other womenfolk, those who had lost husbands when the Cossacks went a-warring. The couple nodded out greetings to people they knew, and now and then stopped to chat for a few minutes. She looked at the children playing in the street and wondered if her first-born would be as energetic, so full of life and laughter. She wondered what he or she would be like when they grew up, what sort of characteristics they would possess? Would they be kind and considerate? Would they say their prayers, like a good boy or girl? Would they have her eyes or her husband's? Would they have her dark hair or his light curls? And although she knew life would be a struggle, she sensed things would be different for her baby, that the times would not be so hard for the working people; that things would change for the better.

The scene shifted.

This time Marfa was laying in bed, her husband's hand pressed to her naked belly, feeling for the baby's kick. The flickering candlelight cast a shadow over his smiling face. The warmth of his touch, his tenderness, and the shared excitement of approaching parenthood so overwhelmed Marfa with happiness, her face became wet with tears again.

'I reckon it's a boy,' said her husband. 'Yeah. I reckon we've got ourselves a right strong little Cossack in there. You can tell by the way he's kicking those legs of his around.'

A knock at the door jolted Marfa out of her dream vision.

She opened her eyes, opened them for real this time, and real tears fell down her cheeks.

'Who is it?' she shouted, trying to disguise the emotion in her voice.

'It's me…Peter. I heard you moaning and groaning, and then a glass smash. It woke me up, it did. Are you all right in there?'

Marfa looked to the floor, where her glass had indeed smashed on the tiles.

Without really thinking, she got to her feet and unfastened the door.

'Oh, Peter! I've just had the most wonderful dream. I was young again and I–' the young lad looked so shocked, Marfa trailed off into silence.

'Marfa…your skin, it's…your wrinkles have all but disappeared.'

Chapter Four

The townsfolk noticed a change in Marfa Orlova. Her skin looked far more youthful; there was a healthy blush to her cheek, that of a woman in the prime of her life. No longer did she walk so awkwardly. In fact, her body seemed completely transformed; much rounder around the hips and stomach. If they did not know any better, they could have sworn Maximov's housekeeper, the stooped, prematurely aged hag, was pregnant.

This did not escape Chernov's attention.

Ever since he left the house yesterday morning, he had been desperate to gain access to Maximov's room. From a vantage point across the street, he watched the guards' movements very carefully. As a familiar and trusted face, he stopped by to offer his assistance and ask about any new developments. Not to have done so, he thought to himself, would have looked out of character. And the more he thought about the wine, the more he wanted to try and get his hands on some.

His curiosity only increased when he saw Marfa Orlova return from the market.

'Marfa! Marfa!' He rushed over and insisted on helping with her shopping bags. 'Please, allow me. You'll do yourself an injury.'

In the morning light, he noticed all the things the townsfolk had been whispering about–Marfa's face bore hardly any traces of her former wrinkles, and her body had a plump, youthful suppleness–she was almost attractive now.

'Whatever has happened to you, my dear? You look like a girl of eighteen.'

Marfa lowered her head, as if ashamed to talk of such matters.

'I've had a visitation, that's what.' She looked warily up and down the street. 'A good demon entered my dreams last night and returned all that was taken from me in my early life.'

'What do you mean? A good demon?'

'Come inside and I shall tell you all about it.'

Marfa had always been a superstitious woman. In all the years Chernov had known her, he could not remember a sensible word ever passing her lips; she was always muttering some ancient prayer and crossing herself. After listening to her story, and all the cryptic allusions to pregnancy and motherhood, he was in no doubt that she was completely out of her mind, that the shock of her master's disappearance had precipitated some sort of breakdown. Who had ever heard of such nonsense, a woman of her age becoming miraculously impregnated, like some kind of belated Mary?

To humour her, he asked various questions, nodded and smiled at the appropriate time, but it was not until she mentioned the wine she had taken from the vat yesterday that he started to really listen.

'So,' he said, putting his cup of tea back on the table, 'you've sampled some of the wine from upstairs, then?'

Once again Marfa lowered her head, as if ashamed of herself.

'I didn't mean to,' she blurted out. 'But when you all left the room yesterday, the wine, it called out to me, it did, telling me to take some.' She wiped some tears from her eyes. 'And when I drank a little in my room last night, I was transported to a magical realm, where all my most precious hopes and dreams were granted.'

'Magical realm? Hopes and dreams granted?' Chernov stared into space for a moment. 'I'm glad you confided in me, Marfa. This is a delicate matter, and one I think we should keep to ourselves for the time being. Clearly this wine is invested with miraculous properties.

To make sure, though, I think I should take a sample myself. That way, we'd know this wasn't some kind of one-off.'

Marfa offered no protest. In fact, she looked pleased to have eased her burden, and agreed to help in any way she could.

'That shouldn't be too much of a problem,' she said. 'We could sneak into the room in half an hour or so, when the guards are due a break.'

As Marfa suggested, the task of entering the room and taking the wine proved incredibly straightforward. An hour after their chat at the kitchen table, Chernov was on his way home, a bottle of wine concealed under his coat.

His house was one of the grandest in town, with a wooden roof, leaded windows and a neat wattle fence. Unlike Maximov, the moneylender sought not only the finer things in life, but order and security, too, something his profession demanded.

He unlocked the front door and walked through to the high-ceilinged dining-room. On a polished sideboard were a set of cut glass tumblers, into one of which he poured some of the wine. Holding it up to the light, he tilted the glass from side to side, before bringing it to his mouth and taking a few greedy gulps.

He smacked his lips.

'Why, that's–that's delicious,' he said out loud. 'I think a few bottles of this will certainly turn my pretty little Ekaterina's head.'

Thoughts of the young woman in question flooded Chernov's mind. The only daughter of Vronsky, the blacksmith, he had had designs on her for several years, ever since her father had run up a few gambling debts in town. As Vronsky was an excellent tradesman, well-thought-of and highly skilled, Chernov was more than happy to offer him some financial assistance. In recent months, however, his gambling had been getting out of control again, and Chernov now held security on everything the blacksmith held dear–his home, business and the tools of his trade. It was only a matter of time before he reneged on their various agreements.

Talk of marriage to his daughter, therefore, had come about

naturally. There was a dearth of suitable young men in a region ravaged by war. Moreover, Chernov was a man of means, if a much older one. Whenever the subject was broached (always in a roundabout way), the two men communicated with a series of knowing winks and nods, nose taps and guarded smiles, things characteristic of all clandestine transactions in these parts.

That brought the matter to Ekaterina herself.

The dark-haired, flashing-eyed beauty was now in her twentieth year. Bestowed of all nature's most potent feminine charms, she had set many Cossack's pulse a-racing, and was not exactly a maiden untouched by human hand, either. To this Chernov turned a blind eye. At his age he could not expect the earth. But it was on matters of a physical nature where his hopes and dreams ran aground. By this time Ekaterina was not so much a skilled coquette as a dark seductress. Whenever she got Chernov alone (and remember, this worldly young girl knew exactly what her father and the moneylender had been discussing), she pressed her body against his, nibbled his earlobes and whispered all kinds of lascivious promises. But, unlike other men who came under her spell, Chernov remained unmoved by her touch. He was impotent. And there was no way the worthy Vronsky would let his only daughter marry a man incapable of providing her with any offspring.

This crushed Chernov up inside.

Over the next few months he visited every doctor in the region. He even ventured all the way to the great capital of Petersburg, but to no avail, his case was a hopeless one, hopeless, because the doctors could find nothing wrong with him.

'Perhaps the physical manifestations of your condition have root in some mental trauma.'

Anxiety was the problem, one renowned specialist concluded, suggesting that this most embarrassing of complaints was all in the poor man's head.

He could not understand it. In his younger days his sexual profligacy knew no bounds. He was seen as a veritable lady-killer, someone who trampled young girls' hearts underfoot. His problems started when his wife died of typhus, only a few years into their union. From then on he spent most of his evenings at the tavern, where he developed a taste for strong drink. In latter years, he desperately tried to ingratiate himself with the local community, especially the more respectable families with daughters to marry off. Behind his complacent exterior, the moneylender still haboured dreams of a normal family life, if not children of his own (which he always considered an encumbrance) then at least a wife, someone to cook and clean, to wash and mend his clothes. And it was for this reason that he had been so struck by Marfa's talk of fulfilling her most treasured hopes and dreams.

These memories troubled Chernov. He reached for his glass and took another mouthful of wine, its soothing properties drawing him into the seat of his favourite leather armchair. He sat back, closed his eyes, and felt a warm sensation ease over his body, like a lover's tender caress.

When he opened his eyes again, he was no longer in his own house, but sitting inside Vronsky's shack, a guttering candle on the table providing the only light. Knelt before him was Ekaterina, dressed in a silken nightgown, with flowers in her hair, and her eyes full of passion.

'This really is delicious,' she said, taking another sip of ruby-red wine. 'You must be the right husband for me, if you bring me such fine presents. Come, my master, take me to bed.'

Only when she stood up did Chernov realize that this was their wedding night; the night he had hoped and dreamed of for so long. Rose petals were scattered across the floor, leading to the back of the shack, where he knew the family slept.

No sooner had he laid her down on the matrimonial bed, pulled the gown over her shoulders, than a molten sexual desire coursed through his veins. Through the night, he took her time and again, twisting her young body this way and that, until she writhed around, screamed out in pleasure, until she planted wild kisses to his face and neck, clawed his back and chest with her nails, and told him how much she loved him.

The scene shifted.

Now Chernov and his blissfully happy young wife were living under his roof. He came home in the evening and there she was, wearing a simple house dress, standing behind the stove, preparing him a fine home cooked meal. As soon as she heard his footsteps, she swung round, wiped her hands on her apron, and jumped into his arms. He felt such joy and happiness enter his heart, he felt as if he was going to explode.

'I love you, darling,' Ekaterina whispered. 'I'll never leave you.'

Chernov jolted upright. He was back sitting in his favourite armchair, his face awash with tears.

Emboldened by these visions, he dashed upstairs, washed his hands and face, splashed on some expensive cologne, and changed into his best velvet dress coat. Back downstairs, he poured some more wine into his glass, tossed it back, and then left the house.

Snow had just started to fall. It was dark and very cold, and Chernov knew that in all likelihood, Vronsky would not be at home at this hour. This was confirmed when he reached his shack and saw a single lantern burning in one of the windows, and Ekaterina's shadow passing back and forth.

He crept round to the rear of the property and tapped on one of the windows.

A moment or two passed before Ekaterina opened it and poked her head outside.

'Who's there?' she whispered.

'It is I,' he whispered back, remaining crouched down and concealed from view.

'Who?'

'Why me...Chernov, of course. Is your father at home?'

'No,' she replied. 'But he's due back in an hour or two.'

'Can I come in, then, just for a moment? I have some very important news.'

It was uncanny. When he sneaked in the back door, everything looked just as it did in his dream vision: there was a guttering candle on the table, Ekaterina's hair hung loose over her shoulders, and she wore a similar kind of nightgown.

'What do you want?' she asked, flashing a smile and playing with a few strands of her hair. 'As you can see, I was just getting changed.'

Chernov looked at her in the candlelight, their imagined night of lovemaking flashing before his eyes.

'I've come for you,' he said so sternly he did not recognize his own voice. 'It's been far too long now. It's time we cemented our union.'

Ekaterina's smile widened.

'Oh, you have, have you?' She rounded on Chernov, leaning very close to him. 'We'll have to see about that, won't we?'

He took her in his arms and planted a passionate kiss to her lips.

For all her bravado, Ekaterina went limp and breathless in his arms. Fortified by the wine and thoughts of finally possessing her, Chernov lifted Ekaterina up and carried her over to the bed.

'Take me, my master,' she panted, pulling her nightgown off over her head. 'Take me now.'

It was then, half undressed, gasping for breath, the object of his fantasies lying before him, urging him on, her milky white skin so alluring in the candlelight, that Chernov felt all his desire leave him.

'Damn it!' He jolted upright and rubbed a hand across his face. 'No! This isn't how it was supposed to be.'

Ekaterina sat up.

'What is it? What's wrong?'

'It's…I–'

'Not again!'

Angry, disappointed, she roughly ejected him from the shack, telling him never to return.

'Only a real man will I take for a husband, not some drunken old reprobate who knows nothing of a woman's needs.'

As Chernov walked home humiliated, the cruel, cold wind of truth lashing into his face, he knew he had to get hold of some more of that wine, an unlimited supply, if need be, his future happiness depended upon it.

Chapter Five

Next morning, Captain Levsky received a telegram from his superiors in Petersburg.

> *Requested delegation now in transit–STOP–in interim–STOP–suggest you sample wine to verify origins–STOP–no doubt this is another case of regional bootlegging–STOP–we take a very dim view of these activities–STOP-and must eliminate them at source–STOP–ensure populace remains pacified–END OF TELEGRAM*

The new day brought a fresh layer of snow, covering the nearby meadow and surrounding forest. The rooftops in the market square glistened a brilliant white; smoke as dark as the sky spewed from chimney-pots. Men in sheepskins broke up ice or shovelled snow from the walkways, while the womenfolk poured boiling water into anything that had frozen solid overnight. Many others went about their business, barely exchanging a word, gathering firewood and provisions, in preparation for more bad weather.

Pogbregnyak walked out of the tavern and looked at the ominous snowflakes that had just started to fall. His skin was grey and haggard, his drink-reddened eyes no more than slits in his fleshy face. He coughed and spluttered, cupped his hands over his mouth and lit his pipe. Over the last forty-eight hours he had been the only person in town to notice Maximov's absence. Rarely had his most valued customer stayed away from the tavern for two consecutive nights, especially at this time of year, when the weather was so prohibitive.

He stared up and down the street, as if hoping to hear the rumble of Maximov's cart, or see the drinker himself stumbling down the road, in need of a hair of the dog that had savaged him.

But the next person he saw was Levsky, buttoned up in his greatcoat, his forage cap already dusted with a little snow.

'Pardon me, Captain,' shouted Pogbregnyak, picking his way across the frozen ground. 'Could I have a quick word?'

Levsky stopped and cast a suspicious glance at the landlord.

'What is it?' he said. 'I'm, er...a little pressed for time at present.'

'Don't worry, this won't take long,' said Pogbregnyak. 'I was just wondering what your troops are doing over at Maximov's place, that's all. Has something happened? 'Cause I haven't set eyes upon Anatoly Vasilevich for the best part of three days. It's not like him at all. Usually, this time of year, you can set your watch by his drinking habits.'

Levsky shifted uncomfortably.

'I, er...believe he's a little under the weather, so to speak. That latest drinking binge has caught up with the old fool. Last I heard he was still sleeping it off.'

This did not sound so unlikely. Drinkers of Maximov's pedigree had been known to take to their beds for days after a particularly heavy spree.

'I see,' said Pogbregnyak, sucking on his pipe. 'But what are your troops doing over there, then? I hear they've been coming and going all through the night. Surely a drunken man lying in his bed doesn't need an armed guard.'

Levsky scowled and checked his pocket watch.

'Er, well, Maximov has been good enough to offer digs to a few of my men, you see, and, er...Marfa is supplying them with provisions.'

This did not have the ring of truth about it. Everyone knew the local garrison was woefully undermanned. And Pogbregnyak had been around liars and deceivers all his life, and knew the face of a man trying to conceal something from him.

'Oh, oh I see. That makes perfect sense.' He smiled blankly, showing off his brown, broken teeth. 'I'll look forward to seeing Anatoly Vasilevich when he's back up and running, then.'

Levsky watched Pogbregnyak walk back towards the tavern, knowing this was the moment wild rumours would no doubt start to circulate.

He then set off in the direction of Maximov's house, meeting Marfa Orlova on the doorstep. He had to look at her twice; the woman did not seem quite as old and wrinkled as he remembered.

'The new guards have yet to arrive,' she told him. 'I've left Peter in charge until I get back from the market.'

Levsky entered the house and walked up the stairs, finding the young man in Maximov's room, staring into the vat of wine, as if transfixed. In an instant, the strong alcoholic fumes assailed Levsky's senses, making him check his step. The whole room, the walls especially, were now bathed in an even deeper reddish glow.

Hearing footsteps, Peter swung round.

'Oh, it's you' he said. 'I was just–' he trailed off and lowered his head.

Levsky walked over to the window.

'Peter, you've stayed at the house ever since Maximov disappeared, haven't you? Have you noticed anything strange going on? Has anyone, to your knowledge, gained access to the room, when the guards have been on a break, for instance?'

Peter's face bore a slightly conflicted expression.

'That I don't know,' he said after a long pause. 'Maybe Marfa has popped her head 'round the door, and–and Chernov, the moneylender, called round yesterday.'

'Chernov?' Levsky ran a hand over his mouth. 'Peter, I want you to do something for me. As Maximov's most trusted friend, I want you to monitor activities in the house. Keep a close eye on Marfa, especially. Something doesn't seem altogether right to me. Perhaps she's taken Maximov's disappearance harder than any of us envisioned. I wouldn't want the misguided woman to do anything rash. You know what kinds of nonsense these superstitious folk get into their heads at times.'

Peter promised to report any suspicious activities direct to Levsky.

'Good lad,' said the Captain. 'And would you be so kind as to fetch the samovar? The cold has got right into my bones this morning.'

While Peter was away, Levsky walked over to the wine and he too stared into the mysterious vat, until he felt dizzy and light-headed and dropped to his knees. From the depths of the glistening wine, something was trying to communicate with him, he was sure of it. A voice, indistinct but alluring, whispered and cajoled, drawing him so close, he almost found himself immersing his head into the vat and lapping away at the wine with his tongue.

Levsky bolted upright, shook his head, stood and straightened.

'For pity's sake, man, pull yourself together.'

With a wary look over his shoulder, he took an empty bottle from his inside pocket, filled it with wine, concealed it under his greatcoat, and walked back over to the window.

A moment later, Peter returned, carrying the samovar on a tray.

'Here you are, sir.'

'Er, that won't be necessary now, my lad. I'm sorry to have troubled you.' Levsky looked out of the window. Two new guards were walking up the garden path. 'I didn't realize how late it was. The relief guards have just arrived, and I must get back to the garrison immediately.'

The garrison stood at the edge of the forest, a short carriage ride from town. Made up of high earthen ramparts, a solitary watchtower, and two barracks with cells below, it once had strategic importance in a region rife with territorial disputes, but now represented no more than a token military presence.

As soon as Levsky returned, all he could think about was that first mouthful of wine. His experience in Maximov's room had filled his head with all kinds of wild premonitions, the likes of which he had mocked Marfa Orlova for only a handful of hours previous. But as soon as he entered the main barracks, he did not get a moment's peace. The cook, a corpulent Muscovite with a lazy eye, knocked at his office door to complain about the monthly food ration, staying for the best part of an hour. Then an orderly ran in, telling Levsky that a corporal had been found dead drunk in town, and needed to be dried out in one of the cells. Then he had to deal with some kind of ruckus amongst the other men, regarding a game of cards and an unpaid debt, which threatened to end in a duel. Each of these middling complaints irked Levsky because it reminded him of just how far he had fallen in life.

In the end, he told his adjutant, Bargin, that he was not to be disturbed, that he had a very important communiqué to compose, and would not be requiring anything else that evening. Only then was he able to slide the lock across his door, and pour some wine into a glass. Still, he did not drink it straight away. He enjoyed a rare moment of silence, leaned back in his chair, and looked at the stone walls and rusted grilles over the windows. This place had become a kind of prison to him over the last few years, and it pained him to think back to how promisingly his military career had begun.

To distract his thoughts, he lifted his glass and held it up to the lamplight, tilting the contents from side to side. A connoisseur of the finer things in life, Levsky knew the difference between a good wine and a bad one, and this looked like some of the finest he had ever seen.

'Right, let's have a little taste.'

That first delicious mouthful transported him in time and place, back to the military academy in Petersburg, where he was a young man again, admiring himself in a full-length mirror. The cut of his elegant uniform told him this was his graduation day; that in a few minutes time he would be standing in front of a hall full of dignitaries as a fully-fledged officer in the Tsar's army. It was not without an exquisite thrill of pleasure that he looked at his handsome face and waxed moustache, the perfect cut of his tunic, the fine leather of his knee-length boots, and the gleaming sabre dangling by his side. He looked every inch the best man in his regiment, that, for the last two years, his superiors had taken him for.

'Levsky, old chap. They're ready for you now.'

The scene shifted.

Now Levsky was striding through a grand banquet hall, cutting a dashing figure in full military attire. A brass band played. The very finest of Petersburg society was in attendance. On either side of the hall, ladies in silken gowns and men in dinner-jackets looked on admiringly. Out of the corner of his eye Levsky caught sight of his father, his own military tunic emblazoned with his many war decorations. Even today, when other parents wore joyful smiles, when mothers were so overcome with emotion they held handkerchiefs to faces wet with happy tears, on what should have been the proudest moment of his life, Levsky's father scowled at his son. His mean, contemptuous eyes, eyes that had terrorized Levsky throughout his childhood, offered up a challenge. All this pomp and ceremony was well and good, they said, but a real solider, a real man, one worthy of the name Levsky, had to prove himself on the battlefield.

All the good feeling the wine had instilled in Levsky soured.

And he found himself back at their Petersburg home, as a young boy again, his father towering over him with a riding crop in his hand.

'You're nothing but a coward and a cheat. Your mother has made you far too soft. Now it's my job to toughen you up.'

He brought the riding crop down across his ten-year-old son's behind with terrible force.

Levsky winced; tears streamed down his face.

He remembered all the times he tried to make his father proud– on the sports field or with excellent examination results–but the old man always remained unmoved. It was as if he could see right through Levsky, right into the depths of his inner soul, and knew he was not a very brave or worthy individual, that he really was soft and spoiled; that thoughts of guns and fighting terrified him.

As he approached manhood, Levsky racked his brains for a moment when he had let his father down, when he had given him a reason to hold him in such contempt. Perhaps it was during the hunting season at their estate. In his seventh or eighth year, Levsky had no stomach for blood and guts; for seeing animals shot or torn from limb to limb. He flinched whenever a rifle was discharged. And he recalled all the trepidation of having to endure it day after day, the nights tossing and turning in bed, dreading the morrow. Most of all he remembered how he confided in his mother, and how she made excuses for him, saying he was running a fever or had a migraine.

From an upstairs window he saw the expression on his father's face when hearing one of these flimsy excuses, the same scowl he wore at the parade many years later.

Ultimately, what troubled Levsky most was that his father's assessment of his character proved correct. When Levsky went into battle for the very first time, an explosion sent him into a paroxysm of terror, he disgraced himself, whipped his horse, turned and retreated, leaving his comrades' side, running away like the most reprehensible of cowards.

His fall from grace thereafter had been swift and emphatic. Within six months he was posted to this obscure region, put in charge of a garrison of only twenty-five men, and left to rot. His father never replied to his letters. And not a day went by when the resentment he haboured towards him did not increase, and poison his heart further. If only he had shown a bit more faith in me, Levsky often thought to himself, if only he had loved me, my life would not have turned out such an unholy mess.

He opened his eyes. He felt sick and breathless; his face was wet with tears.

Grabbing the bottle of wine, he refilled his glass, knocked back a huge mouthful, and squeezed his eyes shut again, willing a more positive vision to rise to the forefront of his mind.

In time it came.

Now Levsky was back on the same battlefield, the theatre of his former disgrace. Only this time, when the shells started to fall, he did not feel the cold hand of terror run up and down his back, he did not feel paralyzed with fear, turn and gallop away, but advanced with all the courage and determination of a true hero, careering straight into the enemy. Teeth bared, sabre raised, he cut down one man after another, leading his troops to a quick and decisive victory.

The dream vision deepened.

Levsky saw himself at yet another parade. The same distinguished personages lined a glittering hall, and the same brass band played a triumphant tune. Once again he was dressed in full military attire, stood in front of the Tsar, receiving a St. Anna Cross.

THE HOLY DRINKER

'You are without doubt one of the bravest officers in the country,' said the Tsar, fastening the award to his tunic. 'Russia is fortunate to have such valourous sons defending her territories.'

The hall erupted in applause.

Levsky turned to face the crowd, where his father was clapping louder and cheering longer than anybody else, pride shining in his eyes.

The elation was such, Levsky passed out in his chair.

All through the night, he kept muttering under his breath, 'I'll show him. I'll show them all.'

When he awoke next morning, his breeches were soaked in urine, his head ached and his mouth was horribly dry. Despite all this, he knew he had to get hold of some more of that wine, an unlimited supply, if need be, his future happiness depended upon it.

Chapter Six

That afternoon, an elegant carriage drawn by a pair of fine Kabarda horses pulled up outside Maximov's house. No one alighted for a good few minutes, which gave the townsfolk ample time to gather in the streets, to stop and stare, whisper and speculate as to the identity of this grand visiting personage.

'Who could that be in such a fine contraption?'

'Maybe the old merchant has finally kicked the bucket?'

'Wouldn't surprise me, after all the vodka he's tipped down his neck over the years.'

'Perhaps that's why Marfa Orlova looks so pleased with herself. She'll kop for the old miser's money now, no doubt. Services rendered, so they say.'

They fell silent when Father Semyon got out of the carriage, followed by a frail priest with a white beard and dressed in a robe and long black vestments. Rarely had the townsfolk seen such a striking figure, and many of them took off their fur hats and crossed themselves.

'Right, Father Zubov,' said Father Semyon, taking the much older man's arm and helping him gain a solid footing on the snowy ground. 'Here is the house I wrote to you about, home of Maximov, a merchant and terrible drunkard, a man whose spiritual corruption was almost complete.'

Father Zubov looked lost for a moment, as if trying to adjust to the unfamiliar surroundings. As he did so, he turned and waved to the townsfolk standing across the street.

'I see the common people are out in their droves,' he said. 'That's a good sign, Father Semyon. Worthy souls are always present at the scene of the Lord's greatest miracles. It's written in the Scriptures, so it is.'

As the two priests walked up the steps leading to the house, the front door creaked open and Peter beckoned them inside.

'Ah, Peter, my lad,' said Father Semyon. 'You got my message, then. And I presume the captain has made arrangements for our visit?'

The youngster shrugged his thin shoulders.

'I'm not sure 'bout that,' he said. 'But he's waiting in the hall now, so you can ask him yourself.'

As soon as they entered the house, Father Zubov went right up to Levsky, took hold of his hands and stared deep into his eyes.

'You look troubled,' he said, his crooked fingers snaking their way around Levsky's wrists. 'You look like a man with something dragging on his soul.'

'No, no, I'm, er…fine,' Levsky gabbled, his cheeks reddening. 'It's an honour to meet you, Father, it really is. But we, er…must speak about the nature of your visit.' Father Zubov let go of Levsky's wrists. 'It goes without saying that I have nothing but respect and devotion for the Church, and that I will do everything in my power to cooperate. But I also have orders from my superiors in Petersburg, who are looking to crack down on the production and distribution of illicit alcohol. Until the delegation arrives, therefore, I've been instructed to allow no wine to leave the house. I trust this will not cause you any inconvenience.'

'That remains to be seen.' Father Zubov's eyes narrowed in his head. 'But let me ask you a few questions. It is now three days since the merchant, Maximov, was last seen, is it not? And when his housekeeper'– he turned and gestured towards Marfa, who had just entered the hallway, and who, on seeing him, lowered her head and crossed herself–'went into his room the morning after his drinking spree, she found in place of the settee on which her master slept a vat of wine.'

'That's correct, Father, but–'

Father Zubov raised a hand, gesturing for quiet.

'And that this vat of wine was of such unlikely size and dimension, there was no conceivable way that Maximov could've installed it himself. In fact, when his housekeeper made up his bed, not an hour before he returned, the room–the settee included–was in its usual state, and there was no sign of any such vat. What does that indicate to you, Captain–?

'Captain Levsky, Father,' he replied, continuing a little uncertainly, 'well, it would suggest that something out of the normal realm of our understanding has taken place.'

'Indeed it does,' said Father Zubov. 'And you stand before me talking of "your instructions", believing that you have some authority over the Holy Church of Russia. Shame on you, Captain. From this moment on, I believe it is you who shall take instruction from me, someone invested with powers far less arbitrary.'

'Well, I–'

The old priest raised his hand again.

'If need be, we will take a small sample back to Father Semyon's lodgings. This wine, this strange gift bestowed upon us by who knows what holy power, may well have healing properties of some kind. There are so many sick and needy people in the region, Captain Levsky, surely you wouldn't want to get in the way of God's work.'

This clearly rattled the much younger man.

'Oh no, of course not,' he said, struggling to form his words. 'The very opposite, in fact. If that's what you require, your, er…Holiness, then I'm sure you could take a bottle or two away with you, as much as you like. What harm can it do? I'll have young Peter fetch some empties from Maximov's kitchen.'

Father Zubov shook his head.

'No need. Father Semyon and I have our own holy vessels, blessed by the Patriarch himself. Now, if you will excuse us. It is time we feasted our eyes upon this miracle of all miracles.'

'Yes, yes, of course,' said Levsky, turning to the others. 'Peter, show our guests upstairs, will you?'

When the two priests entered the room, both had to check their step, such was the renewed potency of the alcoholic fumes emanating from the vat. They stood in silence for a few moments, contemplating the scene. The walls and ceiling were now covered in purple patches of damp, like festering sores on the skin, a wispy, rose-tinted mist hung in the air, and the floorboards had started to peel and curl.

Father Zubov crossed himself.

'We are indeed in the presence of God.'

He shuffled over to the vat and stared into the very heart of the wine, as light from the windows reflected off its gently undulating surface, like so many rubies shining.

'I must confess, Father Semyon,' he said over his shoulder, 'I read your letter with great trepidation, but also with great joy in my heart. The Holy Book tells of such wondrous happenings, but rarely are mortal men fortunate enough to experience something like this firsthand. Truly we are blessed.' He turned and started pacing up and down the room. 'Our world is indeed a strange and beautiful place, complex and full of pain and suffering at times, but never, if we keep faith in our hearts, is the Lord far from our side.

'The events described in your letter put me in mind of many miracles. Who can forget the story of Pasha-the-Leper, the boy who wandered barefoot across our vast nation, who was shunned, kicked and spat upon, who shivered in the frozen wastelands, willing a merciful death that would not come? For Pasha had been touched by the hand of God. Destined to continue on his journey, hungry and destitute, he stumbled upon a gurgling brook. After drinking a little water, he applied some, like a salve to his sores, filled a flask, and once again continued on his way. Only now his afflictions did not trouble him quite as much, he felt rejuvenated and could move more freely. Indeed, he could even bear to feel the icy wind upon his face, and when he came across other travellers, they did not cower or act aggressively towards him, in the way they used to, but offered him food and drink, and spoke in friendly tones.

'When he reached the next watering place, he caught sight of his reflection in a stream, and staring back at him was a handsome youth with bright eyes and beautiful skin. But this young man didn't rejoice in the purity of his new found flesh, he didn't gambol or carouse. No. He understood the nature of this miracle, and went back into the great Siberian wildernesses to seek out those as unfortunate as he had previously been. He put his lips to the mouth of the leper, he touched the faces of those cruelly disfigured, he dressed the wounds of the amputees, for he knew what it was to truly suffer.

'And like that saintly young man, Father Semyon, we must take exclusive possession of this wine and utilize its curative properties for the good of our brothers and sisters. But we must act with utmost caution.' He walked over to the window and stared at the crowds still gathered outside. 'We know all about the peasants' weakness for alcohol. They will, undoubtedly, abuse the privilege, something we must avoid at all costs. Like so many things on this earth, it is up to us, God's envoys, to protect the people from themselves.'

Under his superior's watchful eye, Father Semyon filled six bottles with wine. Every time he dipped the holy vessel into the vat, the swirling liquid shimmered and gurgled, but strangely, afterwards it did not look in any way depleted. In fact, it appeared to be almost overflowing, as if six bottles had been added not taken away.

'Right,' said Father Zubov a little distantly, as if this anomaly had not escaped his notice. 'I think it best we return to your lodgings now. We have all we need for the time being. And I think we would both feel better after having something to eat and drink.'

Father Semyon occupied a modest house on the outskirts of town, left to the Church by a childless and particularly devout couple. His two domestics, a plump old cook and wizened, wispy-haired man servant, took care of the upkeep of the building, carrying on a little farming, maintaining vegetable plots, along with the well-being of twenty or so livestock.

After dining, the two priests sat in Father Semyon's study, either side of the stove. The heat acted like a soporific, and for the last few minutes Father Zubov had been yawning and rubbing his face.

'I fear my fatigue is getting the better of me, Father Semyon, and think it best that I retire for the evening.' He got slowly to his feet. 'It has indeed been a momentous day. And we certainly have many challenges facing us, but I'm confident we will not be found lacking.'

'And how should we best utilize the wine?'

'When the time is right, we will know. Of that I'm certain,' Father Zubov replied. 'Undoubtedly, great changes will take place in both our lives. In the coming weeks and months we will become well-known across all these Russian lands, we will be cherished and revered, spoken of and written about, and many demands will be made of our time.' He nodded gravely. 'But we must not shirk from thought of personal gain, so alien to our Orthodox beliefs. Rest assured. We will be guided by the hand of God. For now, I wish you a good night's sleep.'

'And I you, Father Zubov, I will see you in the morning.'

The day's events weighed heavy on Father Semyon's shoulders. For a full five minutes, he stared blankly into space. Having known his calling from an early age, he had led a simple life, devoted to the Church and his parishioners. But in his darker, more reflective moments, like the one he was experiencing now, he doubted the worthiness of his fellow man. There was so much baseness and inequality in their society. He saw it in the rich landowner beating a peasant to death with a riding crop, as much as in the backward provincial forcing his daughter to become his new wife. It was hard to reconcile the opulence of the Tsar in his Petersburg palaces, with the poverty Father Semyon saw on a daily basis.

These contradictions drew him to animals. There was something pure in the eyes of a devoted dog, for instance, which renewed Father Semyon's faith. Over the years he had built up a reputation as man at one with all God's creatures, having taken in many strays, dogs overworked, abused or neglected. In these pitiful creatures he found a shred of humanity, which made him feel much better about his own place in the world.

He got up and opened the door.

'Eli! Come on, boy, come inside.'

A poor mongrel-setter hobbled into the room, coming to rest at

Father Semyon's feet as he once again sat before the stove. The dog had been so mistreated and malnourished all its fur had fallen from its coat.

Suddenly inspired, Father Semyon reached for one of the bottles of wine, poured a little onto a piece of cloth and dabbed it against the dog's scabrous skin, in the way he imagined Pasha-the-Leper, the hero of Father Zubov's story, had nursed the sick and needy people he came across on his travels.

'Perhaps I'm just being a stupid old fool,' he whispered to himself while pouring some wine into a glass.

Like the others, he did not drink it straight away, but held it up to the lamplight, tilting the contents from side to side, before taking a few sips.

'Why, that's—that's delicious.' He was not sure why he had acted so rashly, but as soon as he drank the wine, he knew he had done the right thing.

Closing his eyes, he saw himself walking through the town square on a swelteringly hot summer's afternoon. It was market day. Crowds of colourfully-dressed people flooded the streets. All the usual shops and stalls were open for business, but there was none of the usual haggling over prices, the latent violence that seemed to define even the simplest process of exchange. There were no peasant women or veterans crippled in the war begging for alms, either. There was a new harmony in the air; a spirit of communality. Red flags hung from the roofs of the two-storey abodes, depicting symbols of hard work and togetherness.

Father Semyon walked around, stopped and observed. The people were truly working for each other, exchanging goods on a cooperative basis. There was no money or gold pieces involved; things which had no real value anyway. And the townsfolk appeared all the happier for it.

Then, much to his amazement, Father Semyon saw dogs walking around on their hind legs, talking in human voices, laughing and joking with the women in their kerchiefs and summer dresses, and shaking hands with men in loosened tunics.

'Good afternoon, Father,' said a mongrel-setter with a thick luxurious coat. 'What a beautiful day.'

'That it is, Eli, my dear old friend, God be blessed.'

Father Semyon walked across the square. Where Pogbregnyak's tavern had previously stood was a beautiful stone church, with a glistening spire and high colourful windows.

He pushed open the door.

Inside those same red flags dominated the far wall. The pews were packed with parishioners, dogs stood side by side with their human brethren, singing in the most wonderful choral voices; the sonorousness of which sent a tingle up and down Father Semyon's spine.

His face became wet with tears.

'It's so beautiful,' he said time and again. 'It's so, so beautiful…'

And he was still mumbling these words when he opened his eyes.

All was quiet back in his study. A candle on the sideboard flickered and almost went out.

Father Semyon looked down. Eli was staring up at him, his nose wet and healthy, his eyes bright and his coat thick and luxurious.

'The wine!' Father Semyon leapt to his feet and ran over to the door, intent on waking Father Zubov right away. 'It's a miracle! A miracle!'

Chapter Seven

Meanwhile, Pogbregnyak was feeling increasingly aggrieved. His two best customers had not been seen for the best part of four days and nights. The takings were down. The only information available was wild and contradictory, concerning Marfa Orlova's unlikely pregnancy, and fanciful reasons why soldiers were guarding Maximov's house. This infuriated Pogbregnyak. Men like him loathed the idea of others knowing something they did not. As a result, he drank and smoked far too much, paced up and down the tavern, stared out of the windows, jumped every time the door swung open, and snapped at Marianka, the skinny young serving-girl whom often shared his bed.

For many years Pogbregnyak had sold strong drink to ruffians, thieves and con artists, and knew when to listen and when to talk. Regardless, he could not help interrupting Igor-the-Fingerless, when the balding, barrel-chested drinker started talking about the events in question.

'What was that you said about Maximov's house?'

Igor lit his pipe with his good hand.

'What?' He exhaled a cloud of smoke. 'You didn't hear 'bout that grand old carriage pulling up outside there yesterday afternoon, and that holy man getting out? I thought it was common knowledge, I did. One thing's for sure, though, something's not right over there, with those soldiers coming and going. I reckon the old man must've croaked. Why else would there be all this fuss and nonsense, eh?'

'Maximov dead?' said Pogbregnyak. 'He can't be. They'd have had to have called Doctor Rimsky, got the undertaker in, and organized a coffin and all sorts.'

'True.' Igor sucked on his pipe again. 'But what 'bout those soldiers, then? Armed they are, guarding the place round the clock. What's that all 'bout?'

For this Pogbregnyak had no answer.

And it was to his great relief that Chernov finally walked in through the door, even if it did take him all of half a jug of vodka before he could stop his hands from shaking, or even begin to speak properly.

'What is it, Vasily Ivanovich?' said Pogbregnyak, drawing him aside. 'You look terrible, like you've seen the devil himself. What's happened?'

Chernov's eyes darted around each bloodshot socket and his hand still shook when he tried to get his glass to his lips again.

'It's that wine, Nikita Pavlovich, that accursed, sublime, wonderful wine.'

Pogbregnyak took a step back and stared hard at the trembling wreck that was, up until a few days ago, the usually unflappable moneylender.

'What wine? What are you talking about?'

'I'm–I'm not sure I even know myself.' Chernov looked to the floor. 'It's all so strange, so preposterous. But I must tell someone about it. If not I'll drive myself mad. Is there somewhere we can go?'

'Of course,' said Pogbregnyak. 'We'll go out back.' He took Chernov's arm and led him across the barroom. 'Marianka, bring us another jug of vodka, will you? We're going to the back room.'

The back room at Pogbregnyak's tavern had been the ruin of many a man. This dingy, windowless space with its scraps and peeling walls had played host to all kinds of debauched events–card games, illicit drinking sessions, and orgies with the most disreputable women in town. This was a place where men had gambled away their homes, their livelihoods, their very souls, a place where their wives paid their debts to Pogbregnyak in the currency of their soft white flesh.

As they sat down at the card table, Marianka brought a jug of vodka through with two glasses.

'Leave us now,' said Pogbregnyak. 'We're not to be disturbed.'

He filled both glasses.

Chernov wiped his face with a handkerchief.

'Nikita Pavlovich, what I'm about to tell you must be kept in the strictest confidence.'

'That goes without saying. I class you as one of my dearest friends, Vasily Ivanovich. If you have any troubles, then consider those troubles halved, as I will do anything in my power to ease your burden.'

'Thank you, that means a lot to me, it really does. Now, all this started the night Maximov brought that wine into the tavern...'

In shaky tones, with sweat pouring down his stricken face, he told Pogbregnyak the whole story, from Maximov's mysterious disappearance, to the vat of wine, and his own experiences when drinking it.

When Chernov had finished, Pogbregnyak leaned back in his chair and rubbed his stubbly chin.

'Are you sure this isn't just one of Maximov's moneymaking schemes? He told us that he bought the wine from a—'

'That's what I thought at first,' said Chernov. 'But believe me, this is no ordinary wine. It holds the key to a man's soul, to his most prized hopes and dreams. And we must gain access to it, to the whole vat if possible.'

Pogbregnyak looked thoughtful for a moment.

'Yes. Yes, we must. Wine of that sort is not easy to come by.'

But it was unclear whether he really understood what Chernov had been talking about. For the landlord, all forms of alcohol possessed magical properties. And the way he responded suggested he was thinking more about stocking his own wine shelf than coming into possession of an elixir that could help fulfil all his wildest fantasies. Then again, men of Pogbregnyak's limited intelligence have just as limited aspirations.

'I'm with you all the way, Vasily Ivanovich. But how are we going to get inside Maximov's room, if armed guards are stationed by the door, night and day?'

Chernov shot to his feet, bristling with so much nervous energy he almost knocked his chair over.

'That's what I've been trying to work out for the last two days.' He started to pace up and down. 'I haven't slept for racking my brains. But not until I ventured over here did a viable plan take shape. As I crossed the market square, I bumped into young Peter. The boy has slept at Maximov's house ever since his master disappeared. When I saw him, he told me he was on his way to visit his sick mother, to spend a few hours at her bedside. What I propose, therefore, is this: we'll go to Peter's shack now, and when he comes out we'll speak to him, and persuade him to help us gain access to the room.'

'That sounds like a grand idea.' Pogbregnyak stood up. 'Come. Let's grab our coats.'

In haste, the two men left the tavern and made their way across the market square.

It was a cold, clear night, not another soul was out on the streets. The snow on the ground had turned to ice, which scrunched under their hurried footsteps.

The Petrenko family, of whom Peter was the only surviving child, was one of the poorest in town. They lived in a miserable wooden shack. The father had been killed during the war, as had two older brothers, leaving Peter and his mother destitute. And this was a perennially sick woman, the kind so common amongst our peasantry, a woman destined for a hard, miserable life.

No sooner had Chernov and Pogbregnyak arrived than the door opened and Peter exited out into the night.

He had ventured no more than a few paces before Chernov called out his name.

'Psst, over here…don't be afraid, Peter, it is only I, Chernov, and Pogbregnyak from the tavern.'

He walked over to where they were standing.

'What are you two doing here?'

51

Chernov flashed Peter his most charming smile.

'We need to talk to you,' he said, beckoning him closer. 'It's about a very important matter. It's about that wine in Maximov's room. We need to sneak a few bottles out somehow, as much as we can manage, and thought you'd be the ideal man to help us.'

Even in the darkness, the look of reluctance on Peter's face was clear to see.

'Oh, I don't know 'bout that,' he said. 'The captain is adamant that no wine should leave the house. Those two priests are the only ones who've been allowed to take any away with 'em. And I wouldn't want to get myself into any trouble.'

Chernov draped his arm around the boy's shoulders.

'But, Peter, we're Maximov's oldest and dearest friends. You know that. And you know he would've wanted us to have had some. Remember that night at the tavern, the night before he disappeared, when he shared all his wine with us? That proves it, does it not? And, as I'm sure you realize, it's no ordinary wine. There's something strange about it, and myself and Nikita Pavlovich are determined to find out what it is. So consider this an act of service to your fellow townsfolk. And we'll certainly make it worth your while.' He took a silver ruble from his pocket and pressed it to the boy's palm. 'That will help you obtain medicines and wholesome food for your poor old mother now, won't it?'

Peter stared at the coin in his hand.

'Well,' he said, lifting his head. 'I shouldn't really, but for the master's friends, I s'pose I can make an exception.' He stole a wary glance over his shoulder. 'The guards always nip off for an hour or so around midnight, it's the boredom that does it, I reckon, so I could easily sneak up the stairs and draw off a bottle or two of wine, but no more. I wouldn't want 'em to notice that any had been taken.'

With this much agreed upon, Peter made his way back to Maximov's house, promising to appropriate the wine and deliver it to Pogbregnyak's tavern at the earliest opportunity.

'That's settled, then,' said Pogbregnyak, as they walked back across the market square. 'What do you want to do now, Vasily Ivanovich, come back and wait?'

Chernov came to a stop.

'No. I shall call back in the early hours of the morning. Be sure to leave the back door open for me, and, under no circumstances should you sample the wine before I get there.'

Well before midnight, Pogbregnyak heard tapping at his back door. When he opened up, he found Peter standing on the step.

'Oh, hello, Peter. You're early.'

'The guards nipped off a few minutes ago. Here.' He handed Pogbregnyak two bottles of wine. 'Take these. I must get back at once. I don't want to rouse anyone's suspicions. Marfa Orlova has been acting very strangely of late, wandering around the house at all hours.'

'Thank you, Peter. You've done the town a great service.'

After bidding Peter goodnight, Pogbregnyak took the wine through to the back room. Having closed up early and sent Marianka to her own bed, the silence, where usually there was whispered conversation and the odd splutter of laughter, felt slightly unsettling. As he waited for Chernov, Pogbregnyak found himself wandering around the room, running his hands through his hair, lost without those familiar distractions. Every so often, he stopped, rubbed his chin, and glanced at the wine on the table. If he did not know any better, he could have sworn the bottles had moved, and that each was possessed with some strange life-force, which seemed to be trying to communicate something to him. This he put down to the vodka he had drunk earlier, but a few glasses had never affected him like this before, causing him to imagine things.

After another half an hour had passed, he answered the wine's persuasive call. Sitting down, he eased the cork out of one of the bottles and poured himself a glass.

'Well, what harm can one glass do?' he said out loud. 'I can always tell Chernov that Peter spilled a little as he carried it over here.'

His excuses already made, he raised his glass to the candlelight and titled the contents from side to side, in just the way he remembered Chernov doing four nights previous.

'Beautiful.' He brought the glass to his lips, closed his eyes, and tossed it back.

When he opened his eyes again, he was no longer in that dingy back room, but in the apartment he shared with his mother during his childhood, watching her at her dressing table, applying make-up, and then brushing her luxurious blonde hair.

As always, she caught sight of him in the reflection from the mirror, turned and smiled.

'What are you doing, creeping up on me like that?' She beckoned him over, picked him up and sat him on her knee.

All kinds of smells, familiar, beautiful smells, assailed his senses: her hair, her perfume, the expensive creams she put on her face, a hint of vodka. A heady combination that, even at his tender age, he knew was refined and sophisticated. It was these things, and his mother's undoubted beauty, that made him think she was some kind of princess.

Over time, this conviction grew.

At night, he was often woken and taken to a neighbour's house to sleep. At weekends, he was shipped off to an aunt, a miserable spinster with a hooked nose and black teeth, who fed him nothing but cabbage soup, and made him sit in a darkened room, all on his own, with no toys, no books, no candlelight, even. To make up for it, his mother took him out after school and bought him bon-bons and all kinds of sweet treats, the likes of which other boys in his class could never afford to eat. On these excursions, well-dressed men, those of importance and position in town, nodded to her respectfully, tipping their hats. There was something in their eyes that made the young boy feel proud of her. Having never known his father, he used to dream that he was just like one of these men—tall, imperious, a little scary, perhaps—and that one day he would come back and they would live together, like the happy families he sometimes saw playing in the park.

The dream vision deepened.

He was older now, back in the same apartment he shared with his mother. Her beauty had faded, her figure was no longer so slender and well-proportioned, her clothes worn and ill-fitting, her make-up, which she used to apply with such care, looked thick and clumsy, almost a clown's mask. A much older man, with a chubby face and greasy hair, was sitting on her bed, telling her to undress.

Pogbregnyak recognized the look in his eyes. It was the same look he saw in the eyes of those well-dressed men as they tipped their hats and muttered pleasantries. Only now, he realized it was not respect that had lit up their faces but sexual desire. He tried to push past his mother. He shouted obscenities at the man, who just sat there, waving his insults away.

'You're being silly, Nikita,' said his mother, looking at him with such sadness in her eyes, it choked him up. 'Go and visit your friends. There really is no other way. You'll understand when you're older.'

She pushed him away and slammed the door shut.

He jolted upright. His face was wet with tears, the back room bathed in darkness, as the candle on the table had burnt out.

Just as he lit another one, he heard tapping at the door again.

He walked over and whispered, 'Who is it?'

'It's me…Chernov. Quickly, open up, it's freezing out here.'

Pogbregnyak unbolted the door.

'My God! Nikita Pavlovich, what's happened to you? You're shaking. You're as white as a sheet.'

Chapter Eight

The rumours that Captain Levsky feared could not be repressed forever. Wild talk soon swept through the town; talk of wine infused with magical healing properties, of Maximov setting up some kind of distribution centre from his house, of guards protecting his merchandise, of all Petersburg talking about his wonderful wine, and how the townsfolk were being cheated out of sampling it.

'We should march right up there and demand a bottle each.'

'It's only right. We're Maximov's neighbours, after all.'

'If anybody should be supping that wine, it should be us.'

But like Pogbregnyak, they did not understand the true ramifications. For them, a wine with magical properties was a strong one which made your head spin and your legs buckle. Their desire to try some, therefore, was based solely on intoxication, of escaping, if only for an hour or two, the misery of their everyday lives.

And just like Pogbregnyak and Chernov, they knew who to go to for information about the wine: young Peter. In the days before the military delegation arrived, the most wily and persuasive locals sought out and harassed him. Whenever the poor boy left Maximov's house he was approached in the same way he had been approached the night before. Those with money offered him similar gratuities— silver rubles, plates of food, vodka, even medicines that might help his ailing mother. Being poor, unused to having money of his own, Peter was an easy target. If only he had been able to resist their advances, what eventually transpired may not have taken place. But by then it was far too late; the townsfolk would not be denied.

In the same way as before, Peter crept up to Maximov's room when the guards had left their posts. And while the young lad may have been many things—with little or no education, he could neither read nor write, the workings of a simple abacus confounded him—of basic common sense, he was not completely devoid. As he drew a bottle of wine from the vat, he too noticed that the level did not seem to drop. He contemplated this for a moment or two. With the wine he took for Pogbregnyak and Chernov last night, surely some dip in the level should have been visible. But no—the naked eye was none the wiser. And like Father Zubov before him, Peter realized that the wine was somehow replenishing itself, that, in effect, there was an inexhaustible supply. This made him feel a whole lot better about his clandestine activities. If nobody noticed, he was free to come and go as he pleased.

And over the next forty-eight hours, that was exactly what he did.

One of the first to take a glass was Gregor Markov, a young soldier who had lost both legs in the war with the Turks. Gregor came from a rich merchant family, one of the most revered in the district, and his disability had broken his father's heart, so active had his only son been prior to his military service. When hearing of the wine's supposed healing properties, he approached Peter, hoping that, if nothing else, a drop of something special would cheer up his gloomy, introspective son, who spent most of his days indoors now, brooding over his misfortune.

No sooner had the first mouthful of wine passed the young man's lips, than he closed his eyes, sunk back into his wheelchair, and imagined himself running through golden fields on a beautiful summer's day. The feeling of exhilaration, the sun on his back, the wind racing through his hair, sent a thrill of pleasure through his whole body.

The scene shifted.

Now Gregor and a friend were wrestling in a clearing to the back of some farm buildings, surrounded by other youngsters from town.

'Go on, Gregor, you've nearly got him.'

'Watch out, Roman, he has a good hold of you now.'

Putting his powerful thighs to good use, Gregor planted his feet and tossed Roman over his shoulders, before jumping on him and pinning him to the dusty ground.

Everyone cheered and shouted Gregor's name.

One of the town's most beautiful girls, Natasha Petrova, walked over and gave him a flower she had just picked from the meadow.

'This is for you, Gregor Fyodorovich,' she said, twining a few strands of chestnut hair around her fingers. 'I hope it brings you luck when you go off fighting those filthy Turks.'

It was then Gregor realized that this was no dream, but a memory of his last few days in town, before he set off for the war, before he was almost ripped in two by an enemy shell.

When he came round, his face was wet with tears, the room, once again, heavy and oppressive in its silence. He looked down, where his strong muscular legs had once been, were the same empty spaces in his trousers, the same scarred stumps that haunted his dreams.

'Father! Father!' he shouted time and again.

The old man dashed into the room.

'What it is, my son? Are you all right?'

'That wine,' he panted, wiping the tears from his eyes. 'You must get me some more of that wine.'

The next reported case was that of Poor Lizaveta, daughter of Pelevin, the finest carpenter in the region. This tragic young woman had been born with a hideous harelip. And few were the townsfolk who did not feel a pang of genuine sympathy whenever they saw her. As from a distance, she looked so pretty, with fine blonde hair poking out of the sides of the bonnet she always wore to shield her face, and with her slender yet well-proportioned figure. How she came to sample the wine was never satisfactorily explained, as she had only just come of age, and was a God-fearing young woman, who, to the best of everybody's knowledge, including her father's, had never allowed a drop of alcohol to pass her lips.

However she procured the wine, she took it to the cottage she shared with her parents and locked herself away in a back room. No sooner had she taken a mouthful, than she closed her eyes and sunk back into an old armchair.

When she opened her eyes again, she was walking around a house full of giant mirrors–the very things she most despised in life, because each time she caught sight of herself it was a hated reminder of her cruel disfigurement. Only now, she did not cower from her own reflection; she walked over and stared at herself with none of the terror and heart-wrenching disappointment of before, because her lip was smooth and unmarked, something which totally transformed her face–she was beautiful now, truly beautiful.

'Hey, Lizaveta!' shouted Mikhail Mikhailovich, one of the handsomest and most popular boys in town. 'Will you come to the dance with me?'

The dream vision deepened.

Now Lizaveta saw herself at one of the famous local dances. From a raised platform a Cossack band played traditional songs, with fiddles and tambourines.

'In thy white hand take it, pray
Please accept it, dear, from me.
Say I am beloved by thee.
What to give, I cannot tell,
To the maiden I love well.
To my dear I think I will
Of a shawl a present make–
Kisses five for it I'll take!'

The sweeping meadow behind the market square was awash with colour. Old and young couples danced and clapped and wheeled around in a blur of flapping skirts and sashaying ribbons. Mikhail Mikhailovich held Lizaveta tightly in his arms. They too twirled around and around. Laughter and the jingle-jangle music, the smell of roasting meats and strong spirits merged into one dizzying whole. Her face became wet with joyous tears; her jaw ached from smiling so much, and she threw back her head and laughed like she had never laughed before, because she was no longer Poor Lizaveta with the harelip, but simply Lizaveta, a normal young woman with the same hopes and dreams of love and laughter as all the other young woman in town.

She opened her eyes, for real this time.

The back room was dark and silent; the evening having crept up on her fast. She touched her disfigured lip, and far different tears rolled down her cheeks.

'I must get some more of that wine,' she whispered to herself, wiping her face with her sleeve. 'I simply have to.'

After Poor Lizaveta came Panchev-the-Poet, an intense young man from a hard-working family, a sensitive soul, with literary aspirations. But no matter how many times he submitted his work to the periodicals, it was always rejected. Like so many others Panchev was inspired by Pushkin. He took pride in the folktales and dances which defined his youth, and wanted to incorporate them into a new, modern style of poetry, written exclusively for ordinary people. He wanted to use his words to inspire them to stand up for their rights; to oppose the ruling classes and grab some land and power for themselves.

In a fit of depression, one familiar to all struggling artists, Panchev purchased a bottle of wine in town and took it back to his gloomy garret, surrounded by pots of ink, paper and books, the only things in the world he possessed.

No sooner had the first mouthful of wine passed his lips, than he closed his eyes and imagined himself standing before a crowd of assembled workers, up on a lectern, reciting his verse:

'In unity we truly rise,
To heights insurmountable,
From the fields and factories
We, the workers, will defeat their lies.'

The men in their overalls and cloth-caps clapped and cheered.

THE HOLY DRINKER

The scene shifted.

Now Panchev saw himself as part of a band of marauding revolutionaries storming the Winter Palace, overrunning the guards, seizing this opulent symbol of the oppressing classes. Gunshots rang out and smoke filled the air. Dead bodies lay strewn across the snow-laden ground.

Men in greatcoats and fur hats, with rifles slung over their shoulders, rushed over to him.

'Comrade Panchev, without your words the workers would never have overthrown the autocracy. You are a true man of the people.'

His comrades hoisted him onto their shoulders.

'Three cheers for Comrade Panchev.'

He jolted upright, gasping for breath.

The light from the candle on the sideboard flickered in the darkness. Panchev leapt to his feet, dashed over to his writing desk and started to fill page after page with his most impassioned verse to date. In the back of his mind, though, he knew the wine had provided this burst of inspiration, and was already plotting ways to get hold of some more.

That Korsakov, the most feared Cossack in town, obtained some wine was inevitable. Nothing escaped the notice of this bear of a man, with his dark curly hair and big bushy beard. Rumoured to have killed more than once with his bare hands, the horrors he perpetrated during the war with the Turks, no sensible Cossack dare speak of. When he worked in the fields he was a fearsome sight, scything down corn with his great muscular arms, doing the work of four or five men. He was just as daunting at the dinner table or in the tavern, eating and drinking with such a voracious appetite it was like watching a wild animal tearing its prey from limb to limb.

The first mouthful of wine transported Korsakov to a golden throne in a palatial palace, with half naked serving girls fussing around him, feeding him great hunks of meat and handing him goblets of wine.

'Would you like some more suckling pig, Your Excellency?'

'Aye, and bring me another pail of vodka.'

A snivelling politician rushed over.

'Your Excellency, we can't possibly declare war on Prussia, England and France at one and the same time. Our forces simply aren't sufficient.'

Korsakov leapt to his feet, turning over the banquet table, bottles, glasses and plates smashing on the floor.

'Silence!' he roared. 'Attack them we will. I myself shall lead our troops into battle. Then the whole world will cower at the mention of my name. Then the whole world will come under the yoke of the Holy Rus!'

When the dream vision dissipated, Korsakov thirsted for more wine, for he knew the more wine he drank, the more powerful he would become.

But of all the people who sampled the wine, none was more poignantly affected than the shopkeeper, Yashin. A keen astronomer, he spent his evenings watching the stars through a telescope he himself had modified. His mind was full of all kinds of radical ideas about man's relation to the cosmos. In notebooks he made detailed calculations, charts and diagrams. If any of his customers were foolish enough to broach the subject, he would regale them for hours with talk of spaceships flying off to explore far-away planets, and of the other life-forms likely to inhabit them.

Well liked, seen as a harmless eccentric, Yashin would sometimes take his books down to the tavern of an evening, occasionally starting up conversations which baffled the other patrons. And it was here he came into possession of some wine, taking it back to his room above the shop.

Here his dream visions were so vivid, so very real. In a white-walled laboratory, he saw himself sitting beside another man in glasses, both scribbling furiously into notebooks.

Yashin stopped writing, took off his glasses and rubbed his eyes.

'What is it?' asked the other man.

'I–I think I've done it.' Yashin put his glasses back on. 'I think I've worked out how to generate enough power to exit the earth's atmosphere.'

The other man shot to his feet and began scrutinizing Yashin's calculations.

'My God! You're right. You've done it! You've actually gone and done it!'

The scene shifted.

Now Yashin saw himself in a protective suit, with some kind of elaborate helmet on his head, standing beside a huge metal projectile, bigger than any boat that had ever sailed the seas.

'Good luck, Comrade Yashin,' said the high-ranking officer standing before him. 'Your work has already proved invaluable. Space travel will truly advance mankind.'

Yashin opened his eyes.

The lamp burning on his writing-desk cast a ray of light over a section of his notes. He got up and scanned his own calculations, and, just like Panchev-the-Poet, was possessed of such a burst of inspiration, he scrawled down page after page of radical formulae, until his wrist felt numb and the morning light was almost upon him.

When finished, he splashed some water onto his face and quickly dressed, knowing he had to open the shop soon. As he busied himself with his clothes, his eyes came to rest on the empty bottle of wine.

'The wine, why of course. I must get hold of some more wine.'

Within a couple of days, more people had sampled the wine than those who had not. And it had devastating effect.

Those desperate to obtain another bottle ran around in an agitated and violent frenzy. Fights broke out in the streets. Those who had not the slightest idea what was going on overheard these miraculous stories, and were eager to find out what all the fuss was about.

This portended badly.

Soon a large group had gathered outside Maximov's house, whispering and conspiring.

Chapter Nine

News of the potential uprising soon reached Captain Levsky at the garrison.

'Captain, come quickly,' said Bargin, bursting in through the door. 'There's been an incident at Maximov's place.'

'Incident?' said Levsky. 'What kind of incident?'

'It's the townsfolk, sir. They're completely out of control, surrounding the place, they are, threatening to knock down the door and take all that wine for 'emselves. The guards have fired off a few warning shots, but still they won't back down.'

'Wine?' said Levsky, as if coming out of a daze. 'Er, have my chaise brought round to the front of the barracks. I'm sure this is no more than a case of drunken high spirits.'

By the time he arrived at the scene, things had almost reached crisis point. A dozen men were standing at the bottom of Maximov's yard, some holding rifles and sabres, others axes and pitchforks. Young boys were climbing trees, trying to get onto the roof.

Levsky alighted from his chaise and dashed over.

'What is the meaning of this?' he shouted. 'Go home, I tell you. There's nothing here for you.'

Korsakov stepped forward of the others, a rifle slung across his shoulder.

'We want some of the wine that's been doing the rounds, that's what.'

'Wine? Doing the rounds?' said Levsky. 'What on earth are you talking about, man?

'Don't try and pull the wool over our eyes, Captain,' said Korsakov, puffing out his considerable chest. 'Half the town has been drinking it. We just want what's our due.'

'I'm afraid you've been misinformed, *sir.*' Levsky tried to stand firm but his cracked voice failed him. 'Now, if you don't return to your homes this instant, I'll have no option but to arrest you.' He took his service revolver from its holster. 'Understand?'

Korsakov did not even flinch.

'Be careful, Captain. People who go 'round waving guns, 'specially those who haven't got the guts to use 'em, usually meet a bad end.'

The two men stood staring at each other.

Levsky was the first to look away.

'Er, well, don't say you weren't warned.' He turned towards the house, saying over his shoulder, 'Now, go home, all of you.'

Trying not to look afraid, he walked down the path and opened the front door.

The first person he saw in the hallway was Marfa Orlova.

'You stupid woman!' He rushed over and shook her by the shoulders. 'Don't you see what you've done? You've caused havoc passing that wine out amongst the townsfolk. Now they'll stop at nothing, not until they've overrun the place and emptied the vat upstairs.'

Peter came running through from the back of the house.

'Stop, Captain.' He tugged at Levsky's sleeve. 'Leave her alone. She didn't do nothing wrong. It's me that's been passing that wine out. I–I couldn't help it. They ganged up on me, offering me all sorts.'

Levsky swung round.

'You?'

Before he could go on, a rock smashed through one of the windows, coming to rest at his feet.

'Sir,' shouted a guard from upstairs. 'The townsfolk are advancing. What shall I do?'

Levsky looked from side to side, as if searching for assistance of some kind.

'Fire!' he cried. 'It's our only hope. They'll tear us to pieces if we don't make a stand.'

A braver, more experienced man would never have acted so rashly. Here a calm head was needed, someone who could talk to the people; negotiate; reach a compromise; reason with them. Sadly, in this regard, Levsky was found completely lacking.

He peered through one of the windows as the rifleman fired a shot into the advancing crowd, hitting Korsakov in the leg. The great Cossack cried out in pain and fell to the snow-covered ground. This startled the others, and they quickly dispersed, carrying the injured man away with them.

The marksman came scampering down the stairs.

'That wasn't a wise move, Captain. Now we've opened fire, wounding one of their own, the townsfolk will never forgive us.'

Within the hour, they had returned in much greater numbers, no doubt incited by stories of the army opening fire on civilians. It was getting dark. Maximov's house was surrounded on all sides and…

The tavern door swung open, bringing with it the sound of swirling wind and a flurry of snow, cutting the old man short. Young Turgenovsky, a gangly youth with curious, different coloured eyes, crept in, no doubt looking for his father, one of the town's most notorious drinkers.

'He's not here,' barked Petrov. He, like many others, had no time for the Turgenovsky family. The old man had a liking for girls not long out of swaddling clothes, and his son, 'cause of those eyes of his, was seen as the devil's own.

'Was he here earlier?' asked the boy, cowering in the shadows.

'Yes, but he's long gone,' said Petrov. 'Now, be off with you. This is no place for a youngster.'

The boy lingered for a moment, before turning on his heels, running out and slamming the door shut behind him, banishing the elements.

The interruption broke the spell of the old man's story.

Volya got to his feet.

'Why are you warning us 'bout the "perils of drink", old man?' he

asked. 'From what you've been telling us that wine did have something magical 'bout it, being able to transport people back in time and place, sending a thrill of pleasure and whatnot through their bodies. It sounds like jolly good stuff to me. What'd you say, boys?' He turned and grinned at the rest of us lads, even his brother, who he was close to hitting with a bottle an hour or two ago. 'I'd say it's time for another drink, eh?'

'You see?' The old man shot to his feet again, a horrible expression twisting his toothless mouth. 'That's typical of the ignorance of youth. You never think 'bout the consequences of your actions; you think a moment's bliss will make up for a lifetime of foolishness. But it doesn't, and never will. No. Life isn't like that, lads. It's a precious thing that must be treated with respect.'

His outburst regained everybody's attention.

'Now, listen and listen well,' he said. 'For I shall tell you how this terrible story ended...'

Why the townsfolk decided against attacking the house that night, when facing minimal resistance, and with experienced riflemen amongst their number, will never be known. Perhaps the earlier gunshot had unnerved them, perhaps they felt more comfortable attacking in daylight, or perhaps they realized the wine was not going anywhere, and it was only a matter of time before they got their hands on it, so why risk further injury? Whatever the reason, not launching a swift counter-offensive proved costly.

At first light, when they tried to enter the house, armed men crawling front first through the snow, their advances were easily repelled. Levsky and the two soldiers inside fired off a series of warning shots which sent the insurgents scurrying for cover.

This was repeated every half an hour, with much the same results.

It was only later, when Korsakov returned to the fray, his leg heavily bandaged, that the townsfolk started to coordinate their attacks, and the house looked to be in real danger of falling. His riflemen took up positions on either side of a raised mound and peppered the building with a volley of shots. In between these bursts of gunfire, children in the surrounding trees hurled rocks at the house, smashing windows, upstairs and down, and other men crept ever closer, some getting as far as the garden path, where they concealed themselves behind sections of the fence still intact.

Inside the house tempers flared. Since nightfall, Levsky and his men had feared an inevitable and decisive assault, and were now running low on ammunition. From their defensive positions, they exchanged heated words, realizing the desperateness of the situation. If the townsfolk gained access to the house, there was no way they would let them live. Surrender was not an option, either. The moment Korsakov had been shot put paid to any chances of an amicable resolution. And of this, they were painfully aware.

'What are we going to do, Captain?' asked Drabkin, the man who had wounded Korsakov. 'We can't hold out forever.'

Levsky, his face haggard through lack of sleep, sweat soaking through his loosened tunic, stood by a window at the front of the house, shaking his head from side to side. Time and again, he cursed himself for his lack of soldierly foresight. Why oh why did I not send someone, young Peter, perhaps, to the garrison to warn the other men, before it was too late?

'Captain? Can you hear me?'

'Of course I can hear you, you fool!' he snapped back. 'We'll just have to hold out for as long as possible. I'm sure some men from the garrison will come to our aid soon.'

'Captain,' shouted the other rifleman from the rear of the house. 'The townsfolk are coming up the back garden. They're almost at the door.'

Levsky ran downstairs, and with the help of Marfa and Peter, barricaded the back door, pushing a heavy chest in front of it.

'Right, Marfa, take Peter to your room and bolt the–'

A volley of rifle shots, unlike those from earlier, cut him short.

'What's that?' he said, fearing the worst. 'That sounds like heavy gunfire.'

He dashed back to the front of the house, and through one of the broken windows watched mounted soldiers race over the brow of the hill leading up from the meadow. It was the delegation from Petersburg, of this Levsky was certain.

'We're saved!' he cried. 'We're saved!'

Sight of mounted soldiers, even if there was only half a dozen of them, was more than enough to frighten the townsfolk. The riflemen disappeared from view. The others dropped their axes and pitchforks to the ground and retreated into the forest. The children jumped from the trees and followed after them.

The military delegation took swift control of the situation. The commanding officer, Lieutenant Belanov, a tall, angular man of fifty, with side-whiskers and a regal bearing, sought out Captain Levsky.

'Who's supposed to be in charge here?'

Levsky, dishevelled, looking like a ghost of his former self, trudged out of the house.

'I, Captain Levsky, am in charge of the local garrison, sir.'

Belanov's eyes narrowed

'What on earth has happened here, man? We were sent to assist in dealing with a matter of regional bootlegging, not help quell an armed uprising.'

Levsky lowered his head and mumbled out a few words of apology.

'It's like a carnival of debauchery,' Belanov went on, ignoring Levsky's gabbled explanations. 'The common people are completely out of control, wandering the streets, either drunk, or so far gone on strong liquor, they're prepared to kill for another drop of the stuff.' He shook his head. 'I think we'd better go inside. I think you'd better tell me exactly what has happened here over the last week.'

As the two officers convened in Maximov's bedroom, Marfa, Peter and the riflemen set about sweeping up the splintered wood and broken glass.

In contrast to those who had recently entered the room, the vat of wine seemed of little interest to Belanov, and he gave it only the briefest of inspections, as he did the dappled walls and peeling floorboards.

'Right, Captain Levsky. I read your telegram. But I think you better give me a more detailed and sober account of the events that culminated in this morning's uprising.'

And he did. He told Belanov about everything surrounding Maximov's disappearance, omitting only details which might cast him in an even worse light.

'And the only witness to all this was the woman downstairs,' said Belanov, 'his housekeeper, the religious fanatic, who can't take two steps without crossing herself, or mumbling some nonsensical prayer?'

'Well, yes, but—'

'But nothing, Captain. Don't you see what's right before your eyes? This merchant, Maximov, was clearly up to illegal shenanigans, trying to produce his own brand of homemade wine. The vat over there proves as much.'

'But, with respect, sir,' said Levsky, 'there are so many anomalies here, things that can't be satisfactorily explained. And rumours are circulating around town about the wine itself. It would appear that those who sampled it have been subject to wondrous visions, which prove it is far from ordinary. Look for yourself! Even the naked eye can tell that there is something special about it.'

'What nonsense!' Belanov spluttered. 'Come now, Captain. You're of fine Petersburg stock; your father is a highly decorated officer. Surely, in your short time here, you've not become infected with these backward notions. You know how superstitious the common people can be. If someone sneezes they think it's an evil spirit trying to escape. For pity's sake, man, pull yourself together. How can an officer in the Tsar's army even think such things?'

A proud look came over Levsky's face.

'I think that way, *sir*, because I too have sampled the wine and can vouch for its mystical properties. If a man drinks some, he is no longer the same man; he is subject to a process of intense self-enlightenment.'

Belanov took a huge intake of breath, puffed out his chest, and scowled at the man standing before him.

'If that's the case, Captain Levsky, then I relieve you of your command on grounds of temporary insanity. My men will escort you back to the garrison, where you will be interned in a cell until you come to your senses. In the meantime, sale and consumption of all alcohol will be banned. In addition, I will have my patrols search every tavern, illegal pot-house, cottage and shack, until every last drop has been destroyed.'

Chapter Ten

True to his word, Belanov conducted a thorough search of all dwellings and business premises. His task was made all the easier as the menfolk, fearing punishment for their part in the uprising, had yet to return from the forest. With rifles poised and sabres rattling, the soldiers tramped over the snowy ground, broke down doors where need be, and carried out their orders to the letter.

As barrels of homemade wine and spirits were smashed with axes, proud women with flashing eyes hissed out their disapproval.

'Just wait till our men come home,' said one old woman, turning her austere but still handsome face to the intruders. 'They'll put you in your place! Bursting into honest folk's homes and destroying their property. It ain't right. You'll pay for this, you hear me?'

The soldiers bowed respectfully then went on their way.

In every subsequent dwelling they encountered new, innovative ways of concealment. Some locals had sneaked the odd bottle, jug or pail into a baby's cradle, others in stables under straw amongst the livestock, or up on the roof struts or inside a stinking outhouse.

Having heard of the order, the crafty, conniving Pogbregnyak attempted to hide most of his wines and spirits in a cellar under the back room. When the soldiers came knocking he acted calmly and cooperatively, saying that he fully understood the need for such measures in light of the morning's unfortunate events, and led the men into the main barroom, where he had assembled a dummy store of alcoholic wares, made up exclusively of barrels of his cheapest wine.

'Where's the rest of it?' Belanov demanded, bringing his face very close to that of the landlord's. 'There's no way an establishment of this size could operate on such a measly stock of alcohol. Men like the missing Maximov would drink you dry in one sitting.'

'I–I don't know what you're talking 'bout, your honour,' said Pogbregnyak, shifting uncomfortably. 'That's all I have, honest it is.'

This stoked Belanov's ire, and he had his men turn the tavern upside down, until they pulled up the back room's dusty rugs and discovered the secret hiding-place.

'Well I never!' exclaimed Pogbregnyak. 'Whatever have you stumbled upon? Who'd have thought it? In all my years here, I never knew I had a cellar.'

Belanov did not even deign to look in his direction.

'Men, retrieve everything from down there and then dispose of it outside.'

The soldiers hauled the barrels and crates out of the cellar, rolled or carried them through the tavern door and onto the market square, where their colleagues waited with axes and crowbars.

Pogbregnyak sidled up to Belanov.

'Your honour, are you sure this is necessary? I mean, couldn't we come to some sort of arrangement, just the two of us?'

Belanov glared at him.

'You're not trying to bribe an officer in the Tsar's army, are you?'

'Well, no, of course–' the first thud of axe into wood cut Pogbregnyak short. 'No!' he cried as gallons of precious wines and spirits spilled out over the snowy ground.

Within twelve hours the town had been ridden of all its alcohol, bar the vat of wine in Maximov's room.

The extent of these sweeping measures deeply troubled Father Zubov, and both he and Father Semyon called round to the merchant's house, where Belanov and his men had stayed overnight, not wanting to risk moving too far from the heart of yesterday's disturbances.

The Lieutenant received them up in Maximov's room.

'Right, Father Zubov, what can I do for you?'

The aged priest did not answer right away. He stood by the boarded-up window, looking Belanov over, as if trying to appraise his character.

'Firstly, thank you for meeting with us, Lieutenant. After yesterday's shocking disturbances, I'm sure you must have many things to attend to.'

Belanov nodded, encouraging Father Zubov to continue.

'We need to talk about Maximov's wine.' He pointed to the vat. 'Now, I know this may sound rather fanciful, but in the last few days certain events have taken place, which prove that the wine has been blessed by God.' He raised a hand, dismissing Belanov's expected interruption. 'So I have come to you today with an appeal from the Church. I fully understand the measures you've taken for the welfare of the townsfolk, but surely you're not thinking of destroying the holy wine, too. It would be a terrible misfortune if we were not allowed to put it to good use.'

Once again Belanov looked close to interrupting, and Father Zubov made another pre-emptive gesture.

'Let me put it slightly differently, Lieutenant.' He walked over to the vat of wine. 'Let me appeal to the more pragmatic side of your nature. In the main, our peasants lead a miserable existence. Even if serfdom has been abolished, they still struggle to survive; illnesses which are easily preventable in the great capitals of Petersburg and Moscow ravage whole communities here. Infant death rates are as tragic as they are indiscriminate. People don't have enough food to eat. They live in pitiful conditions. In many cases their only source of comfort in times of hardship is a devotion to God. These are a very devout people, Lieutenant. So if, for instance, they come to church, listen to a sermon, and drink wine infused with the spirit of the Saviour, if they are told that the wine will bring a little joy and contentment to their lives, their existence will not seem so desperate.

74

Do you not see? We have to give such wretched creatures something to cling on to. And if, out of some misguided sense of duty, you destroy the wine, you will be doing more harm than good.'

Belanov did not say anything for a few moments.

'You speak with great eloquence, Father. And let me preface my stance by saying that I have nothing but respect for the good work of the Church. But, as an officer in the Tsar's army, I must do what I consider to be right by the people, regardless of any long-term considerations. What I saw on my arrival in town assures me of this. Whether the common people derive some spiritual nourishment from this wine is of secondary importance to law and order. What is required now is discipline, an iron fist, because people cannot be encouraged to seek salvation through alcohol–they foster far too much superstitious nonsense as it is. Life, and their continued survival, is not like that. And, as you yourself suggested, notions of this wine having mystical properties is indeed "fanciful".'

Father Zubov's face wore a hard expression, unbefitting of a priest.

'But, Lieutenant, Father Semyon applied some wine to the coat of a mangy dog, a dog so mistreated it didn't look to be long for this world. By morning all its fur had returned, as had its vigour.'

'A dog?'

'Yes,' said Father Zubov. 'So, once again, I appeal to you in the strongest terms: hand the wine over to the Church. Let us use it for the good of the people.'

Belanov crossed his arms and shook his head.

'I'm sorry, Father. Later this morning I will give orders for my men to destroy the vat and dispose of its contents. Any symbol of the last few days debauched events could trigger off a similar uprising as before.'

Father Zubov took a sealed envelope from his pocket.

'If you refuse to see reason,' he said, handing it to Belanov, 'then I must give you this letter from Petersburg. In it you will find explicit instructions, signed by one of your military superiors, to the effect that you must hand the wine over to us.'

There was a knock at the opened door.

All three men turned to see Peter walk in, carrying a samovar on a tray.

'I was told to bring you this,' he said glumly. 'Marfa is preparing a few snacks. I'll fetch them when—' a scream and the sound of smashing glass from downstairs cut him short.

'What on earth was that?' asked Father Semyon.

'Must be Marfa,' said Peter. 'She's not been well this morning. I best go and see if she's all right.'

The three men followed Peter down the stairs.

In the kitchen, they found Marfa lying on the floor in a pool of blood. As shocking as this was, what really took everyone aback was that her face, which had appeared so soft and youthful over the last few days, now looked as haggard and wrinkled as before.

'Marfa, what's wrong?' said Father Semyon, kneeling beside her. 'What's happened?'

'It's time,' she said, gritting her teeth.

'Time? Time for what?'

'The baby. It's coming now.'

Chapter Eleven

Despite Doctor Rimsky's atheism and unconventional views, he had always proved popular with the townsfolk. Over the years this slight, stooped man with his pointy beard and pince-nez had saved babies born blue and unmoving, revived those whose hearts had stopped beating, removed bullets, sewn up wounds, and medicated souls in great pain and discomfort. In short, he had provided essential care to simple country folk, who, a few years previous would undoubtedly have perished.

As soon as he entered Maximov's hallway, he shook the sheepskins from his shoulders, discarding them on the floor, and rushed through to Marfa Orlova's room, where soldiers had been instructed to carry her. The ailing woman lay on the settee, mumbling in prayer, clasping the baby's bonnet she insisted Peter find from amongst her possessions.

The first thing Rimsky did was put a hand to her forehead.

'Oh dear, Marfa, you're burning up.' He took a step back and studied her for a few moments. 'Okay, gentlemen, I think you best leave us now. I will have to conduct a thorough examination of the patient. Please, wait in the kitchen.'

Lieutenant Belanov, Peter and the two priests shuffled out of the room.

Rimsky unfastened Marfa's clothing and carried out a few preliminary examinations, checking her pulse and heart rate, turning the poor woman from side to side, whispering to himself as he did so.

'The stomach is distended...traces of blood from the rear and mouth would suggest serious internal haemorrhaging...temperature abnormally high...heart rate erratic.' He stood and straightened. 'Marfa, how long have you been passing blood like this?'

The poor woman shook her head; tears rolled down her cheeks.

'Have you coughed up blood before?'

To none of his questions did he receive anything more than a grunt or a shrug.

Left frustrated, he walked through to the kitchen, where Lieutenant Belanov, the two priests and Peter stood in wait.

'How long has she been like this?' Rimsky asked.

Peter stepped forward.

'I don't rightly know, Doctor. She seemed all right first thing this morning. She made some tea and a few snacks for our guests here. Then she sort of collapsed down in a heap, she did.'

'I don't mean just today,' said Rimsky. 'I mean over the last few weeks and months. You must've spent a great deal of time in her company, Peter. Did she ever complain of stomach pains or of any abnormal bleeding?'

Peter puffed out his cheeks.

'She was always complaining about something or other,' he said. 'But I never took much notice of it...nor did the master.'

Rimsky nodded and stroked his beard again.

'So, is it true, then, Doctor?' asked Peter. 'Is she pregnant? Is she really going to have a child?'

Rimsky's face could not have displayed more incredulity.

'What on earth are you talking about, boy! Of course she's not pregnant. The woman is at death's door, not about to bring another life into the world.'

'What's wrong with her, then?' said Peter.

'In two words,' said Rimsky, '—strong drink–that's what's wrong with her. I see it so often in domestic staff these days. Whenever the master isn't looking they're knocking back a glass of this or glass of that, sneaking half empty bottles to their quarters of a night, hoping he's too drunk to notice. From the look of Marfa Orlova, I'd say she's been a chronic alcoholic for over twenty years. You recognize the signs in cases like these—the ruddy complexion, the bloodshot eyes, the irregular breathing patterns. Yes. Alcohol dependency of this kind always catches up with people in the end.'

'What are you going to do?' asked Father Semyon.

'Hope that she stops bleeding soon,' Rimsky replied. 'If not, she may not make it through the night. In the meantime, I'll try and make her as comfortable as possible.'

As the drama unfolded at Maximov's house, Pogbregnyak ventured out into the forest to hold a secret meeting with the menfolk still in hiding. Down a narrow path he stumbled into the dense, wild undergrowth, snagging his sheepskins on overhanging branches, and cursing under his breath as he almost tripped and fell to the icy ground.

Halfway down the track, a gravelly voice called out to him.

'Who goes there?'

''Tis me, brother: Pogbregnyak from the tavern. I bring you news from town, and a few provisions to ease your burden.'

There was an exchange of whispers from deep in the undergrowth. Pogbregnyak craned his neck, trying to listen in to what was being said.

From out of nowhere appeared Tomsky, a short, impish lad of eighteen.

'Come on, Nikita Pavlovich, through here.'

The boy led Pogbregnyak to a clearing, where the men had set up a temporary camp. So cleverly had they concealed themselves, no trace of smoke from the roaring fire could be seen from the pathway.

After a few greetings, the men got up from their places around the camp-fire and started rummaging through the sacks Pogbregnyak had brought them.

Korsakov was the first to complain.

'Why haven't you brought us any wine or vodka? That's the one thing we need, to put some warmth back in our bones and to uplift our spirits.'

'No wine? No vodka?' moaned the weasel-featured Nazar Marka. 'What sort of comrade are you? Too stingy to dip into your own pockets when your brothers are suffering in the wilderness. Typical. I never did trust you, you tight-fisted miser.'

So vociferous were the complaints, Pogbregnyak started to fear for his own safety.

'Please, brothers,' he pleaded, raising his hands. 'Let me explain. You know not of the harsh new laws enacted since your flight from town. All your families have suffered at the hands of Belanov and his soldiers.'

'New laws?' said Korsakov, tossing one of the sacks aside. 'What do you mean?'

'Cruel, unjust laws,' said Pogbregnyak, 'laws that have all but put me out of business, laws that will anger any true Cossack.'

They all gathered round to listen to him.

'Last night, those soldiers went on a rampage, knocking on every door, searching every shack and cottage, taking our precious homemade wines and spirits, smashing our barrels and caskets, pouring all that God has made worthy over the ground.' The men winced. 'I myself suffered worst. The soldiers ransacked the tavern, taking all my stock out into the square and pouring it away like dirty water.' Even now the memory choked Pogbregnyak; tears rolled down his cheeks.

The men were so shocked they did not know what to say.

'That's why I sought you out,' Pogbregnyak went on, wiping his face with his sleeve, 'to tell you of the horrors your old 'uns and womenfolk have endured. It's a desperate situation, lads. If we don't make a stand now, they'll be turning us into Chechens, banning all drinking and merrymaking. We'll have nothing left to live for.'

'He's right,' said Korsakov, hobbling around the fire. 'Are we going to allow those heathens to run us out of our own homes, to tell us how to live our lives?'

'No!' the other men roared. 'Never!'

Pogbregnyak shouted along with the others, before slyly planting further seeds in their minds.

'The only drop left in town is that wine at Maximov's house.'

'That be the cause of all this trouble,' said Korsakov.

'Course it is,' Pogbregnyak agreed. 'Why'd you think they sent their soldiers here? Why'd you think they opened fire on us? 'Tis 'cause that wine is special, lads. Young Peter told me that when he drew off all those bottles, it replenished itself, like a natural spring, providing an unlimited supply of pure wine for hard-working souls like us, wine which makes a good man even better.'

'That be true,' said Zakharov, a lean wiry drinker, a regular at the tavern. 'I got hold of a bottle of that stuff, I did, took it out to my shed and knocked back a glass right quick. For a good few minutes, it sent me into a funny little daze. I didn't know where I was or what I was doing. Then I opened my eyes, and as true as I'm standing in front of you now, I was soaring through the skies on the back of a great eagle, up over the snowy mountain tops, looking down on the forests and meadows, the cold wind whistling through my hair. And as we swooped down, the people in the towns and villages looked no bigger than ants.'

'A giant eagle?'

''Tis true, brother,' said Zakharov. 'And I'll tell you something else. I never did feel such a thrill of excitement in all my days.'

'That's nothin',' said Priapikov, a slim, swarthy Cossack with a taste for strong drink, too. 'I drank a bottle of that wine a few days ago. And, just like Zakharov over there, I closed my eyes like I was goin' to drop off to sleep. When I opened 'em again I was walkin' through a big old cave, dead quiet and pitch dark, it was. And I kept walkin' and walkin', for an eternity it seemed like, 'til I came across a clearin' and found all this gold and jewels, glitterin' and sparklin' like a great sea of riches. And I dived in there amongst it all, and started swimmin' like I was in a river, splashin' 'round, great big diamonds and rubies splashin' 'round with me.'

These tales excited the men.

'And what about you, Nikita Pavlovich?' asked Tomsky. 'What visions did you see when you took a drop of that wine?'

'Me? Much the same, lads,' he said, caught up in the camaraderie, feeling as if he could not disappoint them. 'Only I didn't see no giant eagle or river of gold. No. I saw a procession of beautiful women, I did, naked as the day they were born, all at my beck and call. Blonde 'uns with long legs.' The men chuckled. 'Dark 'uns with smooth, tanned skin and flashing eyes, buxom and full of breast. That wine is a truly blessed thing, brothers, and we must make sure we get a hold of it, whatever the cost.'

Cheers broke out.

When they died down, Tomsky asked, 'But what 'bout folk who say those visions turn dark? That they can be full of all a man's worst terrors?'

'Don't listen to 'em,' said Priapikov, launching some spittle into the fire. 'You heard it from me. And I don't tell no lies, God strike me down if I do. There's no harm in drinkin' wine like that.'

'Let's go now, lads,' said Korsakov, grabbing his rifle. 'We'll overrun 'em and take what's rightly ours. Think of it. If we could get our hands on wine that don't ever run out, we'd be well in, we would, we could live it up like the gentry folk.'

'But we must have a plan,' said Pogbregnyak, talking over the excited whisperings. 'Word has it that those priests have been given free reign over that wine, been seen coming and going, they have, their arms laden with bottles.'

'But what 'bout the vat?' said Korsakov. 'A bottle or two is all well and good, but an unlimited supply...'

'True,' Pogbregnyak replied. 'But still, we can't just blunder our way over there now, we'll be cut down by their rifles. No. What we need to do is wait a while, wait for everything to calm down, then take 'em by surprise, when they're least expecting it. There only be a dozen or so of those new 'uns at Maximov's place and 'bout the same again at the garrison. We could easily pick 'em off, one by one, and then keep all that wine for ourselves.'

Throughout the night, Doctor Rimsky stayed at Marfa Orlova's bedside, watching over her in these critical moments, when he feared her life might be ebbing away.

THE HOLY DRINKER

After giving her something to ease the pain, her condition improved slightly, the bleeding abated, her temperature dropped, and her heart rate, while still a cause for concern, levelled out somewhat.

Eventually, she fell asleep.

Every now and then, Rimsky looked around the room; the only place in the world Marfa could call her own. Like a nesting bird, she had gathered a few keepsakes to make herself more comfortable. Still, that this miserable nook, no more than a cupboard, could constitute a home depressed the good doctor to distraction. In his line of work, he saw the worst kinds of poverty and privation–starving children, old women so ravaged by cold, their fingers and toes had dropped off–and that so much inequality could exist in their society infuriated him.

In the early hours of the morning, Marfa stirred.

'Where–Where am I?' she mumbled, looking around, blinking her frightened eyes. 'What's happened?'

Rimsky sat on the edge of the settee.

'Shush,' he whispered, patting her shoulder. 'Don't excite yourself, Marfa. You've not been very well, remember? You passed out in the kitchen. You gave us all a jolly good scare, I can tell you.'

'Passed out?' She raised a hand and felt her flat stomach. Tears filled her eyes. 'And the baby? Did the baby survive?'

Rimsky looked at the poor, deluded woman and shook his head.

'There was no baby, Marfa. All that was in your mind.'

'No baby?' She tried to sit up, but the pain was too great, and she sunk slowly back down. 'What'd you mean, no baby? I felt it here.' She touched her stomach once again. 'I felt it growing inside of me. You can't tell me I didn't. I know well enough what it feels like to be pregnant. Nine children I've brought into the world, I have.'

Rimsky put a finger to her cracked lips.

'Shush. Please, Marfa, calm down. Don't upset yourself. You're a very sick woman. And you must listen to me and listen well. Those pains you felt in your stomach were very probably ulcerative. How long have you been passing blood? How long have you been in so much pain?'

Marfa lowered her eyes.

'I, er…I don't know exactly…for a long time now, ten or more years, I should reckon.'

'Then why didn't you come and see me?' Rimsky shook his head from side to side. 'I could've helped to ease your discomfort. You needn't have suffered like you have.'

'It's God's will,' she said. 'He must've wanted me to suffer, just like I've suffered all my life. No fancy medicine or newfangled potion can do anything 'bout that.'

Such illogical thought, such irrationality appalled Rimsky. That these simple-minded folk were prepared to suffer excruciating physical pain in the name of a God they had no comprehension of, whose existence could not be proved went against everything he most passionately believed in.

'Marfa, I must leave you for an hour or two. Please, try and get some more sleep. You need to build up your strength.'

He stood and reached for the door handle.

'Doctor? You'll bring the baby through to see me when you return, won't you?'

Chapter Twelve

Chernov woke in the middle of the night, suffering with terrible chest pains. He could barely breathe. The glands in his neck throbbed, as did those in his armpits and groins. When he examined himself, the swollen lumps causing him so much discomfort seemed enormous. Moreover, he felt incredibly tired, as if all the strength had been drained from his body. And it was this sense of profound exhaustion, a tiredness no amount of sleep could redress, that troubled him most of all.

He sat up in bed and held out his hands. Even if he concentrated, each one still shook violently. Normally he would have taken a swig of wine or vodka, but all his alcohol had been seized by Belanov's troops.

He let out a deep sigh.

If only I could have a drop of something strong, he thought to himself, that would surely make all the difference.

He lit the lamp on his bedside table, got up, walked over to the mirror hanging from the far wall and stared at his reflection. Whether merely a trick of the light, it looked as if his face had turned a sickly yellow colour. From all sorts of angles, he craned his neck, dipping in and out of the light, trying to convince himself that his eyes were deceiving him.

Terrified, he extinguished the lamp, climbed back into bed, pulled the covers up towards his chin, and waited until the first rays of morning sun filtered in through a gap in the curtains.

As carts started to clatter along the dirt-track outside, the moneylender, wretched and haggard through lack of sleep, managed to wash and dress himself before leaving the house.

Still in an anxious, tender state of mind, feeling as sick and breathless as before, he stepped gingerly across the frozen ground. The sunlight that reflected off the fresh layer of snow stung his eyes. Every sound seemed amplified, sending him into a panic. More than once, he had to stop and grab hold of a fence or wall to support himself. Increasingly paranoid, he was certain all eyes were following his every move, and he started to hallucinate. Other people looked like scary creatures now. Some slithered towards him like snakes, or grew beast-like heads with fearsome teeth and reared up like horses on their hind legs, as if they were about to charge at him. Everywhere he looked he saw danger and hostility, and it was a great relief when he finally reached Doctor Rimsky's house.

A maid let him in, but the doctor, so his wife came down the stairs and explained, was over at Maximov's place, where Marfa Orlova had been taken seriously ill.

Chernov stood in the narrow hallway, staring at Rimsky's wife, a smart woman in a plain morning dress, but her words did not register at all.

She took his arm, a look of concern on her face.

'Why, you look terrible, Vasily Ivanovich. Sit down for a moment. Let me get you a cup of tea or a glass of water.'

'No, no,' he said, shaking his head from side to side, strands of his thinning hair falling over his face. 'I daren't. I haven't been able to keep anything down since yesterday.'

The front door swung open. In walked Rimsky himself, looking just as tired and dishevelled as the moneylender.

'Oh, hello, Vasily Ivanovich,' he said distractedly, slipping his arms out of his sheepskins. 'What can I do for–?' he trailed off, when noticing Chernov's jaundiced complexion. 'My word, you, er…don't look to be in the best of shape, old friend. Perhaps you better come into my office for a moment.'

Rimsky's office had an air of calm and orderliness about it, underpinned by the upholstered walls and the faint, lingering scent of disinfectant. To one side of a mahogany writing desk was a couch for patients to lie upon, on the other a screen behind which those of a more modest disposition could change out of their clothes.

Rimsky asked Chernov to slip off his jacket and shirt, and undertook a few rudimentary checks, the likes of which he performed on Marfa Orlova yesterday morning. Every time he poked or prodded Chernov, or asked him to turn this way or that, the moneylender winced, and looked to be in such acute discomfort, the doctor's brow wrinkled, indicating a clear and worrying prognosis.

When finished, Rimsky sat at his desk and jotted a few things into a notebook.

'Right, Vasily Ivanovich, I must ask you a few questions about your drinking habits?'

'My drinking habits?'

'That's right,' Rimsky replied, straightening his pince-nez. 'How much, roughly, do you drink each day?'

Chernov puffed out his cheeks and continued buttoning his shirt; his shaking hands not escaping the doctor's notice.

'Well, it's hard to say, Doctor. Maybe a couple of glasses of vodka before breakfast, the norm for any hard-working man these days. Then, a bottle or two of wine with my lunch, a few glasses of vodka when I get home, more wine with my evening meal, and then, there's no telling what Maximov and I might get down our necks at the tavern.' He giggled, and felt terribly guilty when noticing Rimsky's disapproving stare. 'Not, er…everyday of course. But, then again, what's the harm? I've never known a good drop of vodka to harm anybody yet.'

Rimsky shifted a little uncomfortably, and tossed his pen aside.

'Vasily Ivanovich, I've known you for more years than I care to remember, and feel that I must be completely frank and up front with you. It would be wrong of me to do otherwise. In my medical opinion, you look to be in the advanced stages of serious liver dysfunction. The yellowing of the skin, the aches and pains, the inflamed glands, shortness of breath, as well as your, er…other long-standing problem– by that I mean your impotency–are all tell-tale signs.'

'What—What do you mean?'

'What I mean is that you must never drink again, old friend. If you persist, I fear you could be dead before the spring thaw.'

To pacify the townsfolk, Lieutenant Belanov wrote a conciliatory proclamation, and had one of his men nail it to a post in the market square.

It read as follows:

To whom it may concern,

Following the disturbance outside the merchant Maximov's house, it has come to my attention that many of the town's menfolk have fled their homes in fear of arrest. In light of the effect this may have on the wider community, I would like to reassure all those involved that no one will be punished for their criminal activities, regardless of their level of participation. I repeat: all men are immune from any form of prosecution, and will be allowed to return to their homes and places of work as normal. All that we ask is that they turn in their weapons at the local garrison, where they will be kept until such a time as the authorities see fit.

It is also my understanding that some amongst their number may have suffered serious injury, with at least one gunshot wound reported. If that is the case, medical assistance will be offered to all those who require it.

But, I must state most firmly, production, consumption and distribution of alcohol in any form are still strictly prohibited. Anyone caught undertaking these illicit activities will be subject to the harshest punishments possible.

Signed: Lieutenant Belanov – On Behalf of His Holiness the Tsar

'Why are you doing this, Lieutenant?' asked his youthful adjutant, Ulitsky, a few minutes before posting the sign in the market square. 'Surely we should mete out the strictest punishment possible, to deter these upstarts from perpetrating similar outrages in the future.'

Belanov shook his head.

'Not this time, Ulitsky. I'd feel a whole lot safer if those men were in a place where I could keep a close eye on them, rather than skulking around the forest, hatching up all kinds of plots.'

'Oh, oh I see, sir,' said Ulitsky. 'I never looked at it like that. Very wise of you, it is, too, sir.'

Word of this unexpected armistice soon reached the men in hiding.

'What'd you think it means?' Tomsky asked Korsakov, as they huddled around the smouldering embers of yesterday's fire. 'D'you think it's some kind of trap? I mean, they're wily old sorts those Russians, ain't they? This could be some kind of trick to coax us out into the open.'

Korsakov puffed on a cheroot before answering.

'Aye, that they are, boy. Best we keep our wits 'bout us, that's for sure.' He exhaled wispy plumes of smoke through his nostrils. 'Then again, if we hide out here much longer, they'll suspect we're up to something and'll send their soldiers in to flush us out.'

The others looked thoughtful and nodded their heads.

'What I suggest we do is this,' said Korsakov. 'We'll send a few men out to see how the land lies, the old 'uns and young 'uns first. That way, we'll know if this is some sort of ruse or not. As for our weapons, we best hide a few rifles out here in the forest, I reckon. When the time comes for us to get our hands on that wine, we can dig 'em up easy enough.'

In due course, those considered of least value to the next uprising were sent back to town, where armed soldiers patrolling the market square awaited them. As promised, none were arrested. After relaying their names, and giving up their knives and axes and a token rifle, they were told to return to their homes until further notice.

'And where are the others?' one soldier asked Tomsky.

'They'll be along shortly,' he replied. 'Those who were injured aren't too sharp on their legs, if you know what I mean.'

When Korsakov and a few hardliners who had suffered injuries finally appeared, Belanov and some mounted guards rounded them up.

'That looks nasty,' said the lieutenant, inspecting the filthy bandages wrapped around the great Cossack's thigh. 'We best get you up to the garrison for treatment. The infirmary is the only place for you right now.'

'What?' said Korsakov, flaring up. 'But you promised none of us would be arrested.'

Belanov raised his hands defensively.

'And I stand by my word,' he said. 'But there's no way you can hobble around town on that leg of yours. It might become infected. Then who knows what could happen? You might have to have it amputated. And you wouldn't want that now, would you? A Cossack with one leg is not much use to anybody.'

Thoughts of losing his leg, of being maimed like young Gregor Markov, terrified Korsakov.

'Oh, right, I see.' He turned to the other men who were in need of medical assistance. 'It's all right, lads. Climb onto the back of this here cart. They're going to take us up to the garrison, to get us some proper medicines and whatnot.'

When all men had clambered aboard, the cart ambled out of town.

As soon as they reached the garrison, they were transferred down to the cells.

'Hey, what's going on?' Korsakov demanded. 'Why are you shoving us in prison? Your lieutenant gave me his word that none of us were under arrest.'

'Of course you're not being arrested,' said the guard, winking and patting Korsakov's back, 'or being kept here against your will. But the infirmary isn't big enough for you all, so it's easier to put you down here, just while you wait to be seen to.' With the barrel of his rifle, he ushered the other men inside the cell. 'Don't worry. You won't be here for more than a week or two.'

'A week or two!' cried Korsakov. 'It's a dirty trick, that's what it is! Just wait until this gets back to my brothers in town, they won't–'

The guard slammed the cell door shut.

Meanwhile, a thoroughly depressed Chernov left his house for a breath of fresh air. Almost unconsciously his legs took him to the market square; in the direction of the tavern he was so used to visiting at this hour. By then it was getting quite dark and only a few people wandered the streets, their heads down and their arms laden with firewood or provisions. The odd cart scrunched its way along the icy track leading out of town. Resigned to their fate, the townsfolk had retreated to their homes, fearful of what misfortune might befall them next.

When the moneylender reached the market square, the last of the men returning from the forest were being questioned by troops. The raggedy bunch of Cossacks cut a pitiful sight, dirty-faced and shivering after spending the best part of two days out of doors.

The sight of Ekaterina, in a lambskin coat and fur hat, stopped Chernov in his tracks. Concealing himself behind a cart piled with manure, he watched her for a few minutes, watched the way she shifted her weight from one foot to the other, and twisted a handkerchief around her fingers. Even from a distance he could see the blush on her cheek and the look of excitement in her dark eyes. But what really crushed the poor man up inside, when he followed the direction of her stare, was that those cherished eyes of hers were fixed on a sturdily-built, handsome young Cossack with curly hair poking out of the sides of his forage cap. On recognizing this, Chernov almost keeled over, as he had on his way to see Rimsky earlier that morning. Because the look on Ekaterina's face was exactly the same as he remembered from his dream vision, when she lay sprawled naked across a bed, writhing around under the weight of his passion, mouthing the words of love and devotion he had so longed to hear.

His heart hammered out a sickly, melancholy tattoo, which momentarily robbed him of breath. He closed his eyes. He could almost taste that ruby-red wine on his lips, the one that invoked such a delicious and vivid fantasy in the first place. With tears rolling down his cheeks, he started back off in the direction of his empty house. All his thoughts turned to the sweet consolation provided by a good long drink, the likes of which he had turned to so often in the past. Most of all, he thought back to the moment he first sampled the wine from Maximov's wondrous vat, and he longed for a second tasting, longed to reenact that memorable scene back at the blacksmith's shack.

Head down, trying to stifle his sobs, he contemplated a life without alcohol, where he could no longer sit in a quiet corner of the tavern and let the drink flow through his veins, soothing his mind of all troubles, taking him off to some dreamy state of blissfulness, where he could imagine himself in the arms of a beautiful young woman like Ekaterina, and know how good it felt to love and be loved in return. To be denied that crumb of illusory comfort, where he was the man he always wanted to be, really scared him, until he was muttering under his breath, the tears almost choking his voice now:

'I think I'd rather be dead than have to spend the rest of my life like this.'

Chapter Thirteen

When the cell door slammed shut, Levsky knew he had reached his lowest point. If only my father could see me now, he thought, with a bitterness that choked him like a hangman's noose. If he had been resourceful enough, he would undoubtedly have taken his own life. But he just lay on the cold bench, wrapped in a rough woollen blanket, looking at the narrow strip of sky through the barred window, accepting his fate, as he had so often in the past. Even if he did kill himself, he knew his father would still despise him. There would not even be relief at his passing, just a lingering regret of him having existed in the first place.

A scurrying sound disturbed his thoughts.

He turned his head and saw a mouse scuttling across the stone floor. It stopped, raised itself up on its hind legs, sniffed the air for any threat of danger, then darted back into its hole. For a moment, Levsky felt a strange affinity with that insignificant creature, because he knew all about fear and retreating to a safe place, be it his room as a boy, the army as a young man, or this out of the way backwater as a complete failure of a soldier.

And it was thoughts of escape that reminded him of Maximov's wine, of that magical moment when he saw such pride shining in his father's eyes. And even though his dream vision soured, he knew that that wine had the capability to take him to a place where the painful memories, the shame, the hurt and humiliation could no longer touch him.

'If only I could get hold of a bottle now,' he repeated time and again, until his eyes felt heavy and he finally managed to drift off to sleep.

Early next morning, Abakumov, a sinewy corporal with a jagged scar running down one cheek, crept into Levsky's cell and emptied a bucket of ice-cold water over his head.

Levsky jolted upright, gasping for breath.

'Get up!' shouted Abakumov, who had never concealed his contempt for his former superior. 'You can't lie in bed all day. You're not lounging around Petersburg with your cronies now.'

'What's the meaning of this?' cried Levsky. 'What on earth do you think you're doing, man? Have you lost your mind? I'll be out of here in a few days, and then it will be you locked in a cell, not me.'

Abakumov sneered at Levsky.

'We'll see.' Picking up the empty bucket, he turned, walked out of the cell and locked the door.

None of the other soldiers respected Levsky. Those with animal instincts sense weakness and cannot help but exploit it. The Captain's unconvincing style of leadership, dithering speech and blanket indecision made him an easy target. Now they took great pleasure in standing outside his cell, mocking him for his part in the siege.

'I hear you were crying like a baby when those peasants attacked with their spades and pitchforks,' said Abakumov, relishing every word. 'Whoever heard the likes of it before, an armed soldier being scared of a few raggedy provincials?'

'You're a disgrace to the army, a coward,' said another soldier.

These words infuriated Levsky.

'I'm no coward!' He banged his fists against the bars on the door. 'I'll show you. I'll show all of you.'

When they had gone, he paced up and down with all sorts of mad, violent and vengeful fantasies playing out in his head. He saw himself beating his tormentors, punishing them in the only way they respected or understood. But when he really thought about confronting them, face to face, he lost his nerve, and that shameful cowardice, the one they had so mercilessly mocked, rose to the forefront of his mind again, and he knew he did not have it in him to hurt another human being, no matter what the circumstances.

Only Bargin showed any compassion, sneaking down to the cells to give Levsky food and cigarettes.

'Don't worry, Captain. I'll get you something special to help you through the night, that I will.'

When the menfolk were locked in the cell next to Levsky's, his situation worsened considerably. As soon as they found out they were quick to poke fun at him, too, shouting obscenities through the walls.

'He ain't so brave now, is he?' said Korsakov. 'Locked up, instead of opening fire on civilians.'

'You should be ashamed of yourself,' Zakharov joined in. 'Only a rotten coward would've given such an order. There were women and children outside Maximov's house.'

'I'm no coward,' Levsky shouted back, banging his fists against the walls this time. 'You were given due warning. You've only got yourselves to blame.'

'What've you been locked up for, then,' said Korsakov, 'if it ain't for cowardice?'

'Shut up!' cried Levsky. 'Leave me alone, will you?'

Not until nightfall was he granted any peace.

In the early hours of the morning, Bargin crept down to the cells again.

'Captain,' he whispered, careful not to wake the men next door. 'I've brought you something.'

Levsky turned over onto his side and rubbed a hand across his face.

'Bargin? What is it? What have you got there?'

Bargin held up a bulging wineskin.

'Some of that special wine from Maximov's place.' He grinned in the darkness. 'I hid it when Belanov's men searched the barracks. Go on. Take it. It's yours. It'll help you sleep.'

Levsky darted across the cell, the blanket falling from his shoulders.

'I don't know how to thank you.' He took the wineskin, just

managing to squeeze it through the bars. 'Why, this thing is positively overflowing.'

Bargin nodded and flashed his teeth once again.

'I was saving it for a special occasion,' he said. 'But I don't reckon I'll have much of an opportunity now. Just make sure you hide it somewhere safe. That way, nobody will be any the wiser.'

'Why of course,' said Levsky. 'And, Bargin, thank you, you're a true friend.'

They shook hands.

Levsky waited until Bargin's footsteps had faded up the concrete stairwell before going back over to the bench. Pale light from the moon crept through the window. It was very quiet; the odd grunt or snore from the adjoining cell the only sound.

He unscrewed the cap from the wineskin and took a great mouthful.

'Beautiful,' he whispered to himself, wiping his sleeve across his chin, and closing his eyes.

When he opened them again, the cell was no longer silent and bathed in moonlight. Now rays of dazzling sun poured in through the window. In the centre of the room, blindfolded and tied to chairs were Belanov, Abakumov, and half a dozen other soldiers, shivering, pleading for mercy, their tunics loosened and drenched in blood and sweat.

'Please, Captain, have pity on us,' cried Abakumov. 'We should never have disobeyed your orders. You're our undisputed commander-in-chief. We'll do whatever you say… anything to make amends.'

Levsky struck him across the face, bloodying his nose.

'Silence!' he hissed. 'You pathetic creatures must pay for your insubordination.' He swooped down and grabbed a handful of Belanov's hair. 'You! You dared to contradict my direct orders, when any fool could see that Maximov's wine was special. Your lack of foresight could prove costly, Lieutenant.'

'What? But I…What are you going to do with us?'

'There's only one solution.' Levsky started to pace up and down.

'Death by firing-squad. Only a bullet can cure scum like you of your ills.'

'No!' shouted Bargin from outside the cell. 'Think about it, Captain. You're the bravest soldier in the whole of the Tsar's army, of that there's not the slightest doubt. You've proved it on the field of battle countless times before. They were fools to have doubted you, that, they've admitted themselves. So don't lower yourself. Show some compassion.'

Levsky walked over to the cell door.

'Not this time, Bargin, old friend. I have to show them who's in command here. I must act with an iron fist. If not, I risk losing the respect of the other men. There's no other option.' He took out his service revolver and walked over to Belanov. 'What I do today is for your own good.'

He put the gun to Belanov's head.

'Goodbye, Lieutenant.' He squeezed the trigger.

The jangle of keys shook Levsky from his dream vision.

It was morning now; real sunlight poured in through the barred window. Still drunk, still feeling the wondrous effects of the wine, he leapt up, concealed the empty wineskin under his blanket, and shuffled over to the cell door.

Footsteps clicked over the stone flooring, but no sound of stirring could be heard from the adjoining cell.

He waited.

When Abakumov appeared, readying his key, Levsky thrust his hands through the bars and grabbed him by the throat, choking him with all his strength.

'Get–Get off,' Abakumov gasped. 'Please…'

In a flash, Levsky managed to snatch the keys from his hand and open the door. Bundling the startled soldier to the ground, he kicked and punched him, knocking him unconscious.

He stepped out of the cell and locked the door behind him.

'Hey, what's going on?' said Korsakov, rousing himself. 'What are you doing out there?'

Levsky stopped outside the other cell.

'Here,' he said, passing the keys in through the bars and dropping them to the floor. The jangle woke the other men. 'There's your freedom, gentlemen. Use it wisely. When news of your escape reaches Belanov, he will not rest until every last one of you is recaptured.'

Levsky dashed up the concrete stairwell and out into the courtyard.

The other soldiers had just risen and were only then setting about their morning duties. Some were still half asleep, yawning and rubbing their eyes, and most failed to notice Levsky's appearance.

'Look!' a private shouted, pointing to the captain, who was then running towards the main gate. 'There's Levsky. He must've escaped somehow.'

The other men ran towards him, their sabres rattling by their sides, but he proved far too agile and alert to restrain, as if possessed of superhuman strength. Every time they had him cornered, he kicked and punched his way past them. Darting under the watchtower, he grabbed a sabre from a fallen soldier and easily outmanoeuvred the others, ducking this way and that, flashing the blade with the utmost skill and precision, leaving two men with nasty stab wounds to the thigh and shoulder respectively. In a matter of moments, half a dozen soldiers lay strewn across the ground, moaning and groaning, their blood staining the snow red.

Another soldier came out of the main barracks, grabbed his rifle and took aim.

'Don't shoot, you fool!' shouted Bargin, rushing over, waving his arms above his head. 'You can't kill an officer, not like this. They'll be hell to pay.'

Taking advantage of their indecision, Levsky started to climb up the watchtower, where he could easily slip over the wall.

As his daring escape seemed all but complete, Belanov's chaise pulled into the garrison.

'What on earth is going on?' he shouted, leaping out. 'Men! Stop him, for pity's sake. Shoot if necessary.'

So concerned were the soldiers with capturing the fugitive, they did not notice the other prisoners creeping out of the cells and through the main gate, running for the cover of the forest.

'Come down, Levsky, you fool!' shouted Belanov. 'You'll be killed.'

By this time Levsky had climbed halfway up the watchtower. They cannot catch me now, he thought to himself, ascending the last few rungs of the ladder. I'm invincible. I'm the greatest man who ever lived. Look at me! I'm the son my father always wanted. I'm cleverer, stronger, faster and more agile than any of these fools. Damn! Why did I not show my capabilities sooner? Just look at me! Look how I can climb and jump and fight with all the skill and bravery I always knew I possessed.

As these thoughts ran through his head, a bullet whistled just past his face, splintering the wooden ladder, making him lose both his grip and footing. Flailing, and despite his best efforts to cling onto the slated roof, he missed and went plunging to his death. Hitting the ground with a thud, it was his blood that now stained the morning snow red.

Belanov rushed over, cursing under his breath.

'The fool!' he cried, crouching down and checking Levsky's wrist for a pulse. 'Why didn't he stop when we told him to? How am I going to explain this in Petersburg? How am I going to explain this to his father?'

He looked at Levsky's face as the shadow of a smile, the smile of a man who had died proving a point to himself, broke out across his bloodstained lips.

'Cover him up…take him away,' Belanov ordered some guards. 'And gather the men outside the main barracks. I want to know how this happened. I'm going to conduct a full investigation. I'll court martial every last one of you if I have to!'

Chapter Fourteen

The menfolk, even Korsakov, who was still nursing his wounded leg, dashed across the snow-laden fields, ducking in and out of the forest, through ditches and over stretches of frozen river. Any moment they expected to hear gunshots and padding hooves, but the drama surrounding Levsky's escape and foolhardy death had been such that considerable time passed before any soldiers gave chase. To further confuse matters, the men did not return to town or stay in the forest for long, but made their way up to Father Semyon's lodgings, concealing themselves in a derelict outbuilding.

Unawares, the two priests were busy packing bottles of Maximov's wine into crates. Inspired by miracles found in the Scriptures, they had made a list of needy people in the region, those crippled or in ill health, those who could no longer provide for themselves, in preparation for visiting each one in turn. Here Father Zubov's motives became a little unclear, so enamoured was he with the idea of making a name for himself, with being synonymous with the miraculous wine's healing properties, by thoughts unbefitting of a man of God.

Much to the priests' delight, the dog, Eli, continued its remarkable recovery, giving them renewed confidence in Maximov's wine. Not only had its coat grown back but its whole demeanour had changed. Instead of the pathetic, woebegone hound dragging itself around the house, waiting only for death, it had been transformed into a lively and affectionate pet with all the energy of a new puppy.

Tears filled Father Semyon's eyes when he tossed the dog a stick in the garden, and saw how it scrunched over the snow, barked and wagged its tail.

'It's truly remarkable,' he said to Father Zubov. 'Who knows what kinds of wonders are at our disposal now? Perhaps this wine can help regenerate the townsfolk, the region, the entire country, fostering a deep love and respect between fellow men, eradicating all inequality and exploitation.'

Father Zubov nodded enthusiastically.

'We can only hope and pray that that is indeed the case,' he said, patting Father Semyon's shoulder. 'What is certain is that we cannot delay any longer. It's time for us to venture out amongst our people, starting with those townsfolk most in need, then spreading our message into the dark wildernesses of our vast country. Our holy mission, Father Semyon, starts this very day.'

'This very day?'

'Yes,' Father Zubov replied. 'Let us pay a visit to the poor widow Petrenko, whom is said to be at death's door. And bring Eli along for all to see. Then they will know the power of which we are invested.'

Back at the barracks, the menfolk's escape sent Belanov into a rage. Pacing up and down the empty cell, he shouted and swore and threw up his arms.

'I want every last one of those men rounded up—alive or dead. Understand? Any soldier returning empty-handed will have me to answer to.'

The troops, some on horseback, some on foot, set off over the very same snow-laden fields. But the fugitives had been very cunning, sending the faster and more agile men out in different directions, making as many tracks in the snow as possible. This baffled the pursuing soldiers, making it look as if each individual had made off alone.

'What shall we do?' asked one young soldier. 'There's no way we can track them all now.'

'I know,' said his colleague, rubbing some snow over his face. 'But I'm not returning to the garrison empty-handed. You heard what Belanov said. He'll string us up if we do. We'll just have to stay out here until we find something.'

As they continued their fruitless search, they left both the garrison and Maximov's house woefully undermanned.

It was mid-morning when Father Zubov's elegant carriage reached the deserted market square. No shops or stalls were open. Only a few grim-faced peasants skulked around in the shadows, with their heads down, carrying firewood or bundles of old newspaper.

'Stop here, will you?' Father Semyon asked the driver. 'I think we best get out and investigate.'

When both priests had alighted, they saw Doctor Rimsky crossing the square.

'Doctor,' Father Semyon shouted.

Rimsky waved and made his way over to them

'Why are all the shops and stalls closed?' asked Father Semyon, without so much as returning the doctor's greeting. 'Where is everybody?'

'It's those awful emergency laws,' he replied. 'Without alcohol, the townsfolk are reluctant to go about their daily activities. If it carries on much longer, I fear for their futures, I really do. I've just done my morning rounds, and most of the older men are lying on their stoves, still sleeping. The youngsters are not much better, moping around their yards. Everybody has become infected with a dreadful lethargy.'

The priests exchanged worried glances.

'And what of Lieutenant Belanov?' asked Father Zubov. 'Is he aware of the situation?'

'That's just it,' said Rimsky. 'He's up at the barracks. Apparently, there was a, er…incident early this morning, where, I'm afraid to say, Captain Levsky lost his life.'

'What?' Father Zubov put a hand to his mouth. 'How did it

happen?'

'An accident, so I was told,' Rimsky replied. 'If only Belanov hadn't taken such drastic measures, all this could easily have been avoided.'

Eli scampered out of the carriage, jumping up and trying to lick Rimsky's hands.

'Hello, boy,' said the doctor, patting the dog's head. 'What's your name, then?'

'Why, this is Eli,' said Father Semyon. 'Can you not remember the poor dog I rescued a few months back? The mongrel-setter, the one that had been cruelly beaten and half starved?'

Rimsky took the dog's head in his hands.

'What? The pitiful creature that had barely any fur on its body?'

'That's right,' said Father Semyon. 'It's a truly wondrous thing. I applied a little of Maximov's wine to its coat and by morning all its fur had grown back, and the dog was completely rejuvenated.'

'Maximov's wine?' said Rimsky, looking up with a doubtful expression on his face.

'Yes,' said Father Semyon. 'That wine is clearly a gift from God. And this very day, Father Zubov and I are to visit some of the townsfolk to put it to good use.'

Rimsky stood and straightened.

'Do you think that's wise?' he asked. 'Two of my patients are seriously ill, both of whom are heavy drinkers. And when I look around this town I see that drink has brought nothing but misery upon it. If you were to exacerbate the current situation by talking up such things, I fear it could only have an adverse effect.'

'And what?' said Father Semyon. 'You feel their predicament has something to do with Maximov's wine?'

'Not directly, no,' Rimsky replied. 'I am, as you well know, a far from religious man. I believe in medical science, in rationality, in things which can be proved beyond reasonable doubt, and can't help but see what is right before my eyes: alcohol is a very dangerous and addictive thing. It can kill, if not respected, it can destroy more than just the physical body, it can destroy the spirit and well-being of an entire town.'

Neither Rimsky nor the two priests spoke for a few moments.

'Well, we best be on our way, Doctor,' said Father Zubov. 'We promised to pay young Peter's mother a visit. Let's just hope everything returns to normal soon.'

In daylight, the Petrenko's shack looked an even more pitiful sight. It stood on wooden piles a few feet from the ground. Its two rooms were sparsely furnished and in terrible disarray; the walls peeling and the floors covered with filthy rags. The first room, leading from the steps outside, housed the poor widow's bed, on which she lay huddled under a thin blanket. In the other room was a broken-down stove, a table, bench and a few ikons. It was very dark, and the stench of sickness and decay, stale water and rotten food hung heavy in the air.

In candlelight, the woman's face looked hollowed out, like a skull. At first, she did not understand what was happening, or who was standing beside her now.

'Peter, Peter,' she kept mumbling, while pushing strands of hair from her eyes. 'You're such a good boy, Peter…God will reward you for that, he will,' before trailing off into a coughing fit.

Father Zubov raised a cup of water to her trembling lips.

'There, there, Pelagea Ivanovna…take a sip of water…that's it…it will help quench your thirst and soothe your throat.'

Only then, on hearing the priest's calming tones, did the woman come to her senses.

'Oh, Father, it's you…it's time, is it? I'm finally going to be put out of my misery. Thank the Lord. Only He knows what torments I've suffered these last few years–a husband and sons killed, no one to provide for me in my sickness, having to send nothing more than a child out to work for a few measly scraps.'

'Calm down,' said Father Zubov. 'You're upsetting yourself.' He touched her cheek. 'You're burning up. When was the last time Doctor Rimsky visited you?'

'The doctor can do nothing much for me now,' she said, '–I doubt he ever could. No. My time is up…the end will be a relief for such a wretched creature as I.'

'Don't talk like that,' said Father Zubov, a strain of impatience in his voice now. 'All may not be lost, even for you, sick as you are.' He turned to Father Semyon. 'Show Pelagea Ivanovna the dog, bring him inside.'

Father Semyon went and fetched Eli from the carriage.

'You see, Pelagea Ivanovna,' said Father Zubov, beckoning the dog over the threshold. 'A few days ago, this dog had no more than a handful of weeks to live.' He patted the dog's head. 'Then the Lord provided us with a vat of holy wine, which offers salvation, a second chance in life, a chance to be healthy, to be able to walk in the fresh air and feel the sunlight on your face once again.'

The sick woman shifted slightly, peered into the darkness and blinked her eyes.

'Dog? Holy wine?' she mumbled. 'What need have I of such things? I'm not worthy of salvation, Father. Look at me! I'm returning to the ground where I came from, the only place people like me are fit to dwell. What do I want a second chance for? To suffer the loss and misery all over again? Not on your life. If my spirit finds a bit of peace, a place to rest for eternity, that's all I can ask for.'

Father Zubov placed a bottle of wine on the table beside her bed.

'Pelagea Ivanovna, you know not what you're saying.' He poured some wine into the same cup as the water. 'Listen. Take a few sips of this wine. If nothing else, it will help to ease your discomfort. Put your faith in it, and what will you lose? Nothing. Do not sample the wine, and what do you risk forfeiting then? Everything. For that glass contains the spirit of the Lord himself. Those that have partaken of a few mouthfuls have experienced many amazing things.' He moved the glass towards her lips again. 'Go on, take a sip.'

Pelagea Ivanovna brushed his hand away.

'But life ain't for us working people,' she said. 'It's for the gentry, the rich folk—everybody knows that. And they have no use for the likes of me, whether I be young or old, weak or strong.'

'No, you're wrong,' Father Semyon interceded. 'There is hope on the horizon. Society is changing for the better. You need only look to the new laws that have been enacted, freeing the serf from the landowner.'

She tried to sit up, shaking her head from side to side.

'That's not true. Lying here has given me time to think things over. And while I ain't got a very good brain in my head, not like those scholars and clever folk'–she winced as another painful breath passed her cracked lips–'I know I'm not long for this world and shall do nothing to prolong it. All I ask is that you look after my boy, Peter. Now old Maximov has disappeared, I fear he'll not get along in life.'

'Of course we will,' said Father Semyon. 'We'll do everything we can to help him. I myself have become very fond of the lad these last few days. But please, Pelagea Ivanovna, take a sip of wine. Move closer to your God.'

She looked at both priests in turn.

'Aye, okay, then. I'll taste a bit of that wine, if it means so much to you. But all I wish for is the end, not to start all over again.'

Across the dark fields, a few soldiers trudged back to the garrison. Wearied by their long and unsuccessful search, the less well constituted amongst them, hungry and frozen to distraction, had reconciled themselves to Lieutenant Belanov's wrath.

They found their commanding officer down in the cells.

'Well,' he said. 'What news of our escapees? I take it you haven't failed in tracking every last one of them down.'

Abakumov, the bruises from Levsky's fists still fresh on his face, stepped forward, as if he wanted to get his punishment out of the way as quickly as possible.

'Unfortunately, sir, they'd split up and we couldn't track 'em down. Some of the other men have set up a camp for the night. That way, they can make a fresh start in the morning.'

Belanov's eyes narrowed. He tossed the wineskin he had found in Levsky's cell onto the floor.

'And do any of you recognize this?'

The soldiers stood there, looking at it for a moment.

'Er, well, it looks like a wineskin, sir,' said Abakumov. 'Maybe it's Bargin's. I've often seen him with one just like that.'

'Bargin, eh?' Belanov rubbed his chin. 'Yes. He was well in with Levsky, wasn't he? And it looks like he provided him with some of that illicit wine.'

'Wine, sir?' said Abakumov. 'Well, that makes perfect sense, then.'

'How'd you mean, man?'

'Well, this morning Captain Levsky was like someone possessed, like a totally different man altogether.'

'And you put it down to the wine, do you, you fool?'

'But you should've seen him, sir,' said Abakumov. 'The way he jumped 'bout with his sabre, climbing up the watchtower, pushing us 'round, like he had the strength of a dozen men.'

'A dozen men?'

'Yes, sir,' Abakumov replied. 'And now you've gone and found that wineskin in his cell, it can only mean one thing: that the wine they found in Maximov's house really does have special powers.'

Belanov scowled and ground his teeth.

'And you all believe this, do you?' he said. 'All these ridiculous stories?'

'Yes. Yes we do, sir,' Abakumov replied. 'And what's more, that's what the townsfolk think, too, and you can rest assured they won't stop until they get their hands on all that wine for 'emselves.'

Chapter Fifteen

Several days had passed since Pogbregnyak's last drink–and now he was really suffering. In the darkness of his back room, he lay stricken by delirium tremens, flitting in and out of sleep, tormented by horrendous visions. Past humiliations rose to the forefront of his mind. Boys who teased him at school crowded round his adult self. Their faces took on ghastly forms, with features twisted and mouths full of sharp, fang-like teeth.

'Your mother's nothing but a whore.'

'Your mother sleeps with dirty old men for money.'

'She's a tart, a floozy.'

'She shouldn't be allowed to walk amongst decent folk.'

These hideous, disfigured creatures started kicking and punching him. Blows deafened his ears and dazed his vision, until all he could hear was discordant shrieks, and all he could see was a blur of flailing limbs.

The nightmare vision deepened.

Now he saw an assortment of men, young and old, big and strong, those who had beaten him in the fist fights of his youth, banging his head against stone floors for attempting to cheat them in some way.

'No, please,' he cried. 'I didn't mean nothing by it.'

In his more mature, reflective moments he thought these beatings had toughened him up, teaching him hard lessons about life, things that had set him in good stead as he grew older. Now he realized that those cuts and bruises had marked him in different ways, turning him into a conniving, hard-faced swindler, a man who would do any underhand deed to get what he wanted, who would betray his best friend for petty gain.

After that he saw all the young women he had mistreated over the years: old conquests, virgins deflowered, women who harboured genuine affection for him, who could perhaps have loved and cared for him, brought his children into the world, girls whose hearts he had broken, whispered sweet promises to, plied with strong drink, even proposed marriage, just so he could get them into bed. He saw the way he had violated not just their bodies but their souls, corrupting all that was good, gentle and worthy in this world, making them as harsh and cynical as himself. Their faces were no longer fresh, soft and youthful, but tired and wrinkled. All joy, love and laughter, hope for a better future, had been forever erased.

And it was the same transformation he saw in his mother's face, from his earliest childhood memories when he took her for a beautiful princess, to when he was older, and saw her as she really was: an aging woman of the night, a cheap whore whose looks had deserted her.

Then, finally, he spied her through a gap in that door again. Only now she looked even older, clumps of her hair fell out before his very eyes, her body in frayed underwear was no longer soft and youthful, but flabby and mottled.

As she pushed the door to, their eyes met.

'You're being silly, Nikita,' she said, lowering her head. 'Go and visit your friends. There really is no other way. You'll understand when you're older.'

She slammed the door shut.

Pogbregnyak jolted upright, gasping for breath.

These terrible visions made his thoughts dark and irrational. In everything he saw some sort of conspiracy against him, from the smallest, most insignificant occurrences. If Marianka, for instance, laid the table with knives and forks, he thought she was planning to attack him, and run off with the last of his money. And without the distraction of work, the customers, the smoke and the holy drink to calm his nerves, there was nothing he could do to put distance between himself and his inner turmoil.

This worsened by the hour.

He broke out in a feverish sweat, had to avoid sharp objects—the very knives he berated Marianka for putting on the table in the first place—for fear of taking out his frustrations on her.

And he was not the only one to suffer.

In the hours after Gregor Markov drank Maximov's wine, his whole outlook and demeanour changed. He washed himself and brushed and parted his thick chestnut hair. For the first time since returning home he became lively and talkative, speaking to his father like the cheerful, respectful young man he had once been. Out in the yard they reminisced about the days before the war, talked of Gregor's horsemanship, drinking bouts and summer days spent by the river, things the old man dared not mention before, because he sensed how painful these memories were to his son, that the ghost of his former self was burdensome to him.

Now, with the promise of more wine forthcoming, Gregor saw a chink of light at the end of a tunnel that seemed forever shrouded in darkness. Even his mother, with whom he had barely exchanged words since returning home, was treated to a glimpse of her old, beloved son. This made the plump, rosy-cheeked woman so happy, she insisted on cooking him something special, baking all the sweet treats he liked as a child. It was as if Gregor, the real Gregor, despite his horrific disabilities, had finally come home.

All this changed when word of Belanov's orders started to circulate.

'What about the wine?' Gregor cried. 'If those soldiers are destroying all alcohol, I'll never get to sample it again.'

His father rushed over.

'Calm down, Gregor,' he said, patting his shoulder. 'I'll do all I can, I'll speak to young Peter, I'll bribe the guards if I have to.'

Gregor brushed his father's hand away.

'Make sure you do. I don't think I can go on living without it.'

When the true extent of Belanov's emergency laws became clear, Gregor sunk further back into himself than he ever had sunk before.

He refused all food and drink, barricaded the door to his room, and shouted coarse obscenities at his parents when they pleaded with him to see sense.

In desperation, his father did everything in his power to obtain some more wine. He befriended the guards, put word about town that he was willing to pay any price for a bottle or two from Maximov's vat, but no one was prepared to go against the tyrannical Belanov.

Next morning, Gregor wheeled himself outside to watch the young children playing in the snow, dashing around on sledges, their laughter ringing in the cold, crisp air. All the joyful sadness of reliving a treasured memory through somebody else's eyes, eyes that once belonged to him in his boyhood, overwhelmed him.

His face became wet with tears.

Brushing them away with his sleeve, he wheeled himself along the snowy track, past children too absorbed in their own activities to notice, until reaching the brow of the hill leading down to the meadow. It was a very steep drop, already populated with daring young lads on sledges. Gregor angled himself over the precipice and pushed himself down the slope, shouting and laughing, just like the disbelieving youngsters finally taking notice of him. In a flash, he whizzed over the snow, his arms raised, whooping and hollering, a pure exhilaration rushing through his veins.

Back at the Markov's cottage, his father had just noticed his absence.

'Where on earth has Gregor got to?' he asked his wife.

Two young lads burst in through the half-opened door.

'Come quickly,' one panted. 'It's your Gregor…there's been a terrible accident.'

The old man rushed out after the boys.

At the bottom of the hill, surrounded by weeping children, in a mess of twisted spokes, lay his son's legless corpse. Old man Markov turned him over, and, just like the face of Captain Levsky, the shadow of a smile, the smile of a man who had died proving a point to himself, broke out across his bloodstained lips.

Fate was no kinder to Poor Lizaveta. With no wine to cushion reality, she too stopped eating and sunk into a gloomy listlessness, the likes of which can drag a person to the very brink of insanity. For days, she locked herself away, thinking only of that ruby-red elixir and how special it had made her feel, because, for the very first time, she was just like everybody else.

Now and then, those remembered visions—the house of mirrors, her beautiful reflection, whirling around in Mikhail Mikhailovich's arms, the music, clapping and laughter—brought a smile to her face, and she almost lost herself again. Then a barking dog or the wheels of a cart scrunching over the icy roads outside disturbed her thoughts, and she raised a hand to her lip, felt that ugly scar, and broke down, burying her face in a pillow, sobbing uncontrollably.

Her misery was compounded late one night when she heard her parents talking of a miraculous operation performed in Petersburg.

'Yashin, the shopkeeper, told me 'bout it,' said her father, presuming his daughter was sleeping. 'Apparently they take some skin from another part of the body and sort of graft it on somehow, making the lip look normal, without so much as a suggestion of a scar.'

This lifted Lizaveta's spirits.

Next morning, she rose early, dressed, and performed her household duties with all the cheerful diligence of before.

Her father, much relieved, commended her on her high spirits.

'Well, Father,' she said, 'I overheard you talking last night, and want to try and be a good daughter before my trip to Petersburg.'

His face dropped; his eyes filled with tears.

'But, Lizaveta,' he said, 'there's no way we can afford to send you to Petersburg for that operation. Those specialists cost the earth, they do. I'm terribly sorry, child, really I am. If there was anything I could do to help put your face right, I'd do it, I'd give my own right arm'—he rolled up his shirtsleeve—'but it's just not possible. We'd need the help of the Tsar himself.'

The colour left Lizaveta's face. For a moment, it looked as if she too would break down in tears.

'I know, Father, and I'm truly sorry. Having heard you speaking last night, I presumed some miracle had been bestowed upon us.

It serves me right for eavesdropping. I–' she trailed off, and, head lowered, walked to the back of the cottage where she stayed for the rest of the day.

Beside herself, she pounded her balled fists against the cushions on the settee. I would be better off dead, she repeated time and again. Why can only the rich afford such wondrous things? Am I not human, with two arms and legs, skin and bones, just like them? What makes them so special, eh? Well, if we cannot afford such an operation, then perhaps I can carry it off myself.

In this desperate frame of mind, she crept into her father's shed, took one of the smaller chisels–a sharp implement with a silvery point–from a hook on the wall, and, with the aid of a piece of broken mirror, started to hack away at her lip, digging the sharp end into her skin, spilling her blood, until everything went blurry before her eyes.

When her father discovered her, it was already too late.

'Lizaveta, what have you done?'

Things took yet another tragic turn when Panchev-the-Poet called round to see Bunin, the retired schoolmaster. Bunin received the young man in his study with bookcases built into the walls, containing over five thousand volumes, many of them prized first editions. After forty years of teaching, and a lifetime fascination with the written word, he had often looked over Panchev's verse. Only this time, when the old man shook his bald head, and offered a far from complimentary critique of poems composed while the young poet was drunk on Maximov's wine, Panchev was in no mood to listen. Stung by the criticism, feeling all the frustration of an artist, a man ahead of his time, a man destined for great things, he lost his temper, his face turned a horrible purple colour, his eyes darted around under lids swollen through lack of sleep, through hours of artistic endeavour, chasing down phrases he thought to be as important as they were immortal.

'You know nothing, old man,' he said with such contempt in his voice, Bunin stopped speaking, and looked at him with a shocked expression on his face.

'There's no need to be insulting, Yuri Borisovich. Remember, there is an art to taking objective criticism, criticism that is well-meant, that will help you become a better writer. At present, you still have much to learn. And it's not the poems that are the problem here. Your rhyme structure, use of imagery, and the evocativeness of your words are powerful. It's your subject-matter that is at fault. People don't want to read about men and womenfolk sweating in the fields. They want to read about romance, a gurgling brook or a stunning sunset. It's such a shame, because there is a lovely flow to your writing.'

'What am I to do, then?'

'If I were you,' said Bunin, 'I'd write a sonnet for your sweetheart.'

'But I haven't got a sweetheart,' Panchev flared up, '—nor do I want one. This country, these people are the things that inspire love in my heart.'

'But poetry should be about art and beauty—'

'What do you know of art and beauty?' Panchev cried, snatching up a sharp letter opener and plunging it into Bunin's neck time and again, blood pouring over pages of the poet's treasured verse.

How the alarm was raised was never known. But when armed militia burst into the study Panchev was said to be still hunched over the old schoolmaster's body, wearily jabbing the letter opener into wounds which had been inflicted countless times over.

Across town, Yashin, the shopkeeper, was enduring his own personal crisis. After closing up for the day, he retired to his room to look over calculations he had formulated when drunk on Maximov's wine. Only now, his findings, every neat stroke of his pen, looked ridiculous to his eyes, lacking in the kind of foundation all good scientific work is rooted in. He went over his formulas countless times, crossing things out, only to reinstate them in the margins, until each page was a messy hotchpotch of scribbles and ink-blots.

He stood up, banged his fists against the walls, smoked a whole packet of cigarettes, tugged at his beard, and ran his hands through his thinning hair.

'No, no, no....it can't be,' he mumbled under his breath. 'How could I have been so wild, so speculative, so far from the mark?'

It was then he realized that it would take decades, maybe a

hundred years or more, before scientific advancements would make space travel possible. The kinds of metals needed to withstand the requisite temperatures had yet to be alloyed, let alone tested. And most of his calculations about exiting the earth's atmosphere had no basis in fact.

Tears of frustration rolled down his cheeks.

The notes spread before him constituted the dreams of a boy-man who had never really grown up. His life's-work had been an extension of his childish doodles. And at that moment he saw himself as he really was: a lonely bachelor hurtling towards middle age with all the velocity of the rockets he dreamed of inventing, without a single person in the world to care if he lived or died.

This crushing vision darkened.

Now he could clearly picture his own funeral, a cheap coffin being lowered into the ground, a priest reciting a prayer, but not a single mourner standing beside the grave.

And it was this image which saw him lose faith in his dreams.

Wiping his eyes, he gathered up all his notebooks, bundled his way out of the back door to the strip of waste ground to the rear of his shop, and dumped them on the snow. Dashing back inside, he grabbed some kerosene and a box of matches, intent on destroying startling scientific advancements that would take decades for those who followed him to rediscover.

He poured the kerosene over the notebooks, lit a match, and set his work ablaze.

Doctor Rimsky came rushing down the street, having just visited Poor Lizaveta's cottage. The fire caught his eye, and he stopped in his tracks, to see the shopkeeper shivering before the flickering flames

'Yashin,' he shouted. 'What on earth are you doing? Put a coat on, man. It's twenty-below out here....you'll freeze to death.'

All over town there were stories of similar disturbances, where usually mild mannered folk had been acting out of character, either attacking family or friends, or doing harm to themselves or their livelihoods. It was only a matter of time, therefore, that someone as unbalanced as Pogbregnyak finally snapped.

For hours he had paced up and down the back room, not once responding to Marianka's polite questions regarding his evening meal, or what he wanted to do about relighting the stove. All he could think about was Maximov's wine, and ways in which he could procure some more. His temples throbbed. Poisonous energy coursed through his veins. And once again, his beady eyes were drawn to all sharp and dangerous objects.

'Nikita Pavlovich,' said Marianka, 'would you like to try some soup now?'

He swung round and lashed out at her, knocking her halfway across the room.

In a blind rage, he beat her time and again, stamping his feet on her cowering body. After each blow her bruised and battered face took on the form of one of his old tormentors or lovers, and finally, as it looked as if he had killed the poor defenceless girl outright, he saw, very clearly, the face of his mother, the older, uglier, wrinkled version, covered in thick layers of make-up.

'You whore! You sleep with dirty old men for money. You're a tart, a floozy. You shouldn't be allowed to walk amongst decent folk.'

A passing soldier saved Marianka from a certain death. Having heard her scream, he rushed in through the tavern door and managed to push Pogbregnyak away from her.

'Leave her alone, Nikita Pavlovich,' he said, taking his service revolver from its holster and waving it in the air. 'I'll shoot if I have to.'

This returned Pogbregnyak to his senses. He looked at Marianka, lying in a pool of blood, put his trembling hands to his face, dropped to his knees and burst into tears.

But perhaps the most shocking incident took place at the Petrenko's shack. That night, on returning home, young Peter struggled in the darkness, feeling his way over to his mother's bed and lighting one of the lamps.

'Mother?' he whispered. 'I've managed to get hold of some more medicine, the stuff that helps you breathe better.'

As she was lying on her side with her back to him, he reached out and tapped her thin shoulder–it was freezing cold to the touch.

When he turned her over, he reeled so far back he bashed into the far wall, for all the flesh had disappeared from her face and all the hair fallen from her skull–she really was no more than a skeleton now.

He dropped to his knees, mumbling in prayer.

It took several minutes before he had calmed down sufficiently to take everything in, and before he noticed the empty bottle of wine standing on the table beside her bed.

'What?' He picked it up and held it over the lamplight. 'How did she get hold of this stuff?'

It was then a strange expression twisted Peter's face, because he knew his mother's last wish had been granted, that she had been allowed to die in peace, after all.

Chapter Sixteen

Prior to Maximov's disappearance, the biggest threat to the townsfolk's health had been their superstitious beliefs. If Doctor Rimsky performed an operation or prescribed a medicine, therefore, he tried to explain things in simple terms, and when the benefits became appreciable, people soon forgot about these outdated notions. They recognized progress, and began to trust Doctor Rimsky's medical advice. No longer did women chew on hair during childbirth or men toss back three glasses of vodka to cure hiccups.

But in all his years in practice, Doctor Rimsky had never dealt with so many cases of physical injury or temporary insanity. Nearly every household had experienced some kind of crisis, and with so few menfolk around, it fell on the harassed physician's shoulders to provide support and advice.

And in the last twenty-four hours he had barely slept a wink.

When he entered the Petrenko's shack, he found young Peter sitting by his mother's bedside, mumbling to himself, wringing his hands, displaying all the signs of someone struggling to deal with their loss.

'Peter, what ha–?'

'Take a look at her!' He shot to his feet and pointed to the bed.

When Rimsky got a closer look at what remained of the poor widow, he too reeled back against the far wall.

'Dear God!' He put a hand to his mouth. 'How long has she been like that?'

'She was all right this morning. Well, she was still sick, just like before, but she weren't all withered away.'

Rimsky leaned over the bed and examined the skeleton.

'It's impossible! This level of decomposition takes weeks, months, even.' He pulled the filthy blanket lower. 'Hang on. What's this?'

He picked up the lamp and angled it over the bed. Just under the ribcage, where the stomach should by rights have been, was a dark-red stain on the feather mattress.

'It's that wine.' Peter thrust the empty bottle under Rimsky's nose. 'See. Those two priests gave it to her—they must've done.'

Rimsky took the bottle, turned and straightened.

'What?' He stared at it as if it was something completely out of the ordinary. 'The fools! She was far too weak to be drinking alcohol. It could have killed her outright.'

'Weak she may've been,' said Peter. 'But it shouldn't have eaten up all her skin, made her hair drop out, and turned her into a bag of bones now, should it? It's not natural, I tell you!'

Rimsky put the bottle on the bedside table.

'No, Peter, it isn't natural.' He sighed deeply. 'And I'm afraid to say, I've no logical explanation for it. But your mother was in great pain and discomfort, so please, take solace from fact that she's no longer suffering.'

Neither spoke for some time. Rimsky because he was lost in thought, Peter because he was sobbing and wiping tears from his eyes.

'That wine!' he said finally. 'What's so special 'bout it, eh? Why's it making people act so strangely?'

'Again, Peter, I have no answer for you. Drink has always caused many problems in our society. The working people, especially, seek solace in alcohol, an outlet, an escape from their everyday lives, a way they can let off steam and forget about their troubles.'

Peter sniffed and wiped his eyes again.

'So, in a way,' he said, 'it does have something magical 'bout it, 'cause it has the power to take a person away from 'emselves for a bit?'

Rimsky's face bore a conflicted expression.

'I suppose, "in a way" it does,' he conceded. 'But you can't keep going to some magical well whenever things don't work out for you. It's unsustainable. The body can only take so much. In my opinion, the working people would be much better off without alcohol. It poisons the mind, becomes addictive, takes hold of you, until you care about nothing else, not your family, work or beliefs, the only thing you live for is another drink.'

Both fell silent again, the strong wind rattling against the windows the only sound.

'I don't understand all this,' said Peter. 'When's it going to end?'

'That I don't know,' said Rimsky, putting his arm around the boy's shoulders. 'We can only hope and pray that nobody else gets their hands on that wine. If the menfolk were to come into possession of it, I'd hate to think what disasters might befall them.'

Far-away, across the meadows and fields, the soldiers from the garrison continued their search, venturing deep into the forest, scouring the wintry countryside, and interrogating people from nearby villages. Never did they think to look at the priest's lodgings, even though to many, considering the holy men were the only ones in possession of the wine, it was the most obvious place.

At the garrison, Belanov was sure the men had ventured much further a field this time, something that, on reflection, did not seem like such a bad thing. Regardless, he sent a telegram to an adjoining province, asking for a small battalion of reinforcements to be dispatched, informing his superiors of all that had taken place since Levsky's untimely death, and the need to stabilize the situation in town.

For their part, the men in hiding were now restless, hungry and chilled to the bone. The priests had not returned since morning, and the fugitives' patience was getting the better of them.

'Come on,' said Korsakov. 'Let's march up to the house and take what's rightly ours.'

Creeping across the icy yard, they burst in through the kitchen door. Despite the sudden appearance of a gang of ragged, dirty-faced intruders, the old housekeeper and man servant barely rose from their seats at the table. Both acted with complete resignation, as if they recognized the wine's importance, and knew, therefore, that someone would come calling for it soon.

'Easy now,' growled Korsakov. 'Where is it? Where's the wine those priests have been hiding?'

'Through there,' said the woman, showing more weariness than contempt, 'in the pantry. There's three or four cases out there, more than enough for you ruffians.'

'Zakharov,' said Korsakov. 'Go and check.'

Zakharov ducked out of the room, returning a moment or two later with a bottle of wine in each hand.

'Two or three cases!' he beamed. 'There must be all of fifty bottles through there.'

The men needed no further encouragement.

They tied the grey-haired domestics to chairs, and then raided the pantry, grabbing meat pies, chicken legs, pickles and preserves, and all kinds of sugar-coated pastries, things they rarely, if ever, could afford to eat themselves.

Taking their booty through to Father Semyon's study, they huddled around the stove, sprawled out on the floor or in soft leather armchairs. Each man commandeered a bottle for himself, and they took turns in warming themselves in front of the flames, tucking into the food and gulping back the ruby-red wine.

'Cor!' said Nazar Marka. 'This is the proper good stuff. Almost worth getting ourselves arrested and run out of town for.'

'That it is,' said Korsakov. 'And remember, lads, there's plenty more where that came from! No more working or slaving away for us, now we've got ourselves an unlimited supply of this here wine.'

The men raised their bottles, shouted and cheered.

Over the next hour they ate and drank ferociously, each trying to outdo the other, their coarse language and raucous laughter colouring the air. Every time a bottle was emptied, they tossed it to the floor, where it either smashed, or joined the big pile of chicken bones and cigarette butts that had steadily accumulated.

'We've never had it so good, lads,' said Priapikov.

'I could get used to all of this,' said Zakharov, flashing a wonky, drinker's smile, 'that I could.'

As faces reddened and speech slurred, a strange, almost imperceptible hush descended on the room, like mist falling over a river. In the moments that followed, each man's spirit drifted out of his real body, took a step to the side of the room, and watched his real self continue to knock back the wine and devour the food. Bizarrely, not one of the men felt afraid or alarmed by this. In fact, it felt like the most natural thing in the world, as if they had entered a calm and blissful realm of intoxication, ascended to a higher plane, a veritable palace of wisdom.

'What shall we do now?' asked Korsakov, with a tranquil smile on his face, turning to the new versions of his comrades.

'I reckon we should round up some women,' said Zakharov, 'that's always a sure way to liven up a party.'

From out of the misty haze appeared a dozen young women, dazzling in their beauty, dressed in fine silks, like princesses from an ancient fable, with hair flowing past their shoulders.

'Will you get a look at that,' said the spirit of Korsakov, nudging the spirit of Zakharov in the ribs. 'They're proper beauties, they are.'

The women walked over to the real men, touched their faces, held them close, and pressed their lips to their cheeks.

'It's as if we can make a wish,' said Zakharov, rushing down another mouthful of wine, 'and whatever we wish for will come true.'

'What about music, then?' said Korsakov. 'A gypsy band?'

From the same misty haze, a band of musicians in smart tunics and leather boots shuffled into the room, bowed to their hosts, took up their instruments, and started to strum fiddles and balalaikas, shake tambourines, and sing the rousing songs all Cossacks love best.

THE HOLY DRINKER

"'Twas the fair-faced lad got the maiden fair,
Her right hand so white, in his own he took,
And leads her, leads her round the ring.
"Have you, comrades,' he says, "in all your life
Met a lass so sweet as my wife?"'

The women took the men by the hand and started to dance around the room, twirling around in time to the music.

'Look at 'em go, lads,' shouted the spirit of Korsakov, pointing to their real selves and clapping his hands. 'Look at 'em go!'

'Drink and be merry,' said the spirit of Priapikov, jigging on the spot.

'Yes,' said Korsakov. 'Let's open another bottle, eh?'

Many more bottles of wine suddenly appeared—over a hundred lined up by the stove—although no one was sure who had brought them through, or how their number had multiplied.

Regardless, the men drank and drank, splashing through the puddles of wine now covering the floor, almost up to their ankles. Whenever they put an empty bottle down it miraculously replenished itself, or if it fell to the floor and smashed, a new one entirely would take its place. The music got louder, the dancing more frenetic, until everything swirled in and out of focus, until the men were so dizzy and drunk, they fell onto their backsides, and struggled to get back to their feet, splashing around in puddles of wine, like children splashing around in the river.

'Come on, Korsakov,' said Zakharov, trying to drag the great lumbering giant to his feet. 'I think it's time we found you a bed.'

Korsakov got up, wobbled and swayed, droplets of wine poured down his face.

'You might be right, old friend,' he said. 'But I need one of those fine young beauties to tuck me in, though.'

A pretty blonde girl, who could not have been more than seventeen or eighteen years old, stepped in between Zakharov and Korsakov, smiled and took one of his great hands in hers.

'Are you ready, my master?' she said, guiding him out of the room. 'I think it's time we spent some time alone.'

Back in town, the early morning light struggled through a dark layer of cloud. There was no wind in the freezing cold air, only a pervasive stillness; an emptiness almost, in bearing with yesterday's terrible and unexpected events.

Into this strange, stilted atmosphere stepped Doctor Rimsky and young Peter Petrenko.

'I think it's best you come back with me,' said Rimsky. 'My wife will get you something wholesome to eat, and then you can rest up for a while. I'm sure you're exhausted. I'll have her make a bed up for you.'

Peter, his head lowered, mumbled out words Rimsky took for agreement.

As they reached the dirt-track leading to the market square, they saw Poor Lizaveta's parents talking to Gregor Markov's father. Each looked pale and drawn, their eyes red and puffy through all the tears shed overnight.

Rimsky and Peter came to a halt.

'Why couldn't she just have been normal, eh?' said Lizaveta's father. 'Why did God have to curse her like that? It wasn't fair. For parents couldn't have asked for a kinder, sweeter, more dutiful daughter.'

'That she was,' said Gregor's father, patting him on the back. 'It's like my boy, Gregor. There wasn't a braver, stronger Cossack round these here parts. Why'd that shell have to land on him, ripping him in two?'

The doctor looked on sadly for a moment, before ushering Peter forward.

'Come on,' he said. 'Let's go. We'll catch our deaths if we don't get indoors soon.'

Across the street, the local militia was dragging Panchev-the-Poet out of Bunin's cottage. There were marks in the snow, like wheel tracks, where the young scribe had dug his heels into the ground.

'Get off me,' he cried, trying to struggle free, his face red and contorted. 'The Revolution is coming. Holy Revolution! Beloved Revolution! Bread! Land! Freedom to all workers! Let me go, you fools. Don't you see? They've got us fighting against each other, brothers. A hard rain is going to fall. I'm the only one who can help the workers rise up!'

Finally, the militia managed to shove him in the back of a prison carriage.

Up ahead, outside the tavern, Rimsky and Peter ran into Polya Antipova, who sometimes took care of people in town or up at the garrison, when Rimsky was called away to an adjoining province.

'How is Marianka?' he asked.

'Still sleeping,' she replied. 'After the draught you gave her, she dropped right off, the poor thing. Her face is still a right mess, though, and I'm sure she's broken some ribs.'

'We'll know more when the swelling goes down,' said Rimsky. 'I'll call round in an hour or two to check on her. Such a shame for one so young.' He sighed and stroked his beard. 'And what of Pogbregnyak? Where have they taken him?'

'Straight to hell, for all I care.' Polya shook her head and puffed out her cheeks. 'Well, I'll see you later, Doctor. I best be getting back to her now.'

She turned and walked back inside the tavern.

'Doctor,' said Peter. 'I just remembered. I've forgotten something and must go back home to fetch it.'

Rimsky looked at him questioningly.

'Can't it wait? I don't really like the idea of you being there on your own.'

Peter had already started off on his way.

'It'll only take a minute,' he said over his shoulder. 'I'll catch you up.'

When Korsakov finally awoke, he could recall little or nothing from the night before. All that remained was that wonderfully warm, blurry feeling of waking intoxication, when so much alcohol is still present in the bloodstream a man is, to all intents and purposes, drunker than he was when he passed out.

Korsakov stumbled into the study and drew back the curtains, letting bright morning light flood the room.

He rubbed his eyes and turned away from the window.

Nazar Marka and Zakharov were lying on the floor like soldiers wounded on a battlefield. The rugs were covered with wine stains, so too the walls, as if someone had run in with a bucket of the stuff, splashing it all around.

'Wake up!' shouted Korsakov, prodding each man with the toe of his boot.

They started to rouse.

'What happened?' said Zakharov, rubbing his face. 'Where am I?'

'Only the Lord knows,' said Nazar Marka, yawning and blinking his sleepy eyes. 'What a night, eh?'

'Cor, yeah,' said Zakharov, sitting up and leaning his weight on one elbow.' How'd we manage to get all those womenfolk here, and that band?'

'I don't rightly know,' said Nazar Marka. 'Someone rode out on one of the horses. Well, I think they did.'

'Yes,' said Zakharov. 'Now you mention it. I do recall something of the sort happening.'

Korsakov roared with laughter.

'Well, a man knows he's had a good night when he can't remember the half of it.' He yawned and scratched himself. 'I think we best go into the palour and have ourselves a glass or two of that wine, just until we feel better.'

'I've already looked,' said Priapikov, ducking into the room. 'It's all gone. We must've drunk our way through the lot.'

Korsakov stopped laughing, and cursed himself for having been so greedy as to leave not a drop for the morning, when a proper drinking man needs alcohol most.

THE HOLY DRINKER

'Not to worry,' he said. 'We'll head straight into the forest for our rifles. I think it's time we paid Maximov's place another visit. And believe me, lads, it won't end up like last time. You have my word on that.'

Chapter Seventeen

All was quiet at Maximov's house. Two guards in shirtsleeves sat at the kitchen table, smoking cigarettes, playing cards and drinking tea.

'You've got the luck of the devil, you have, Dmitry.'

'That ain't luck; it's skill,' he said, chuckling and rubbing his hands together. 'Go on, Pavel, deal us another hand. It looks like we're in for another quiet day.'

The back door crashed open. In rushed Korsakov and his men.

Dmitry reached for his service revolver.

'Not so fast,' said Korsakov, jabbing a rifle into his back. 'Put your hands where I can see 'em.'

The raggedy bunch of fugitives brought with them the smell of wine and strong tobacco. All were ruddy-cheeked and bleary-eyed, and had that dangerous aura that surrounds men under the influence of alcohol, one that tells others to beware.

Both soldiers recognized this.

'That's right,' said Korsakov as they raised their hands. 'Now, where are the rest of you lot? There are usually more than two guards hanging round this place.'

'Still out looking for you, I should think,' said Dmitry. 'The Lieutenant gave orders for the men not to return to the garrison until they'd captured the lot of you.'

Korsakov threw back his head and laughed.

'You hear that, lads.' He grinned at the others. 'Looks like we've got the whole place to ourselves, then. Right. Best we have a nice long drink.' He turned to Priapikov. 'Tie these two up, good and tight.'

The door adjoining the kitchen inched open and Marfa Orlova poked her head into the room. The men swung round, and were so shocked by her appearance–the snow-white hair, gaunt features, wrinkled face and wasted body–they just stood staring at her, as if she was a ghost.

'What you lot be wanting?' she managed, struggling for breath. 'I won't be having no violence in this house.'

'We've come for the wine, Marfa,' said Korsakov, stepping forward, his rifle now slung over his shoulder. 'We won't be troubling no one, not unless they try and stop us.'

Marfa's bloodshot eyes deepened in her head.

'You fools!' she cried. 'It be evil, that wine. It'll turn brother against brother. Mark my words. If you come to rely on that stuff, it'll ruin the whole town.'

Korsakov waved her words away.

'Be quiet, woman! Go back to your room. You're sick. Anyone can see that. You'll catch the death of cold if you keep wandering around in your petticoat.'

Marfa shook her head, crossed herself, went back inside her room, and locked the door behind her.

'Right, lads,' said Korsakov. 'Let's get ourselves upstairs.'

By this time Maximov's room was enveloped in a thick swirling mist. The walls had blackened like bruised nails. The floorboards were sticky underfoot, oozing with a dark mushy liquid. The air, even though the boarded windows emitted draughts of chill wind, was heavy with alcoholic fumes. While the wine itself still sparkled like the rippling surface of a ruby-red sea.

'Will you take a look at that,' said Korsakov, kneeling by the vat, like a penitent before the cross. 'It's right beautiful, it is.' He stared into the wine, transfixed.

And there he remained, until Zakharov tapped him on the shoulder.

'Are we going to get stuck into that stuff, then?' he asked, turning and winking to the rest of the men. 'We've got a right good thirst on, we have.'

Korsakov stood and straightened.

'Aye, that we are,' he said. 'Marka, bring up some of those empty bottles from downstairs, and then go and round up the other men from town. We'll have a few glasses to put ourselves right. Then we best work out how we're going to guard this old place.'

Inevitably, a few glasses turned into a few glasses more, until the men were crowded around the vat, dipping their bottles into the wine whenever they pleased. Much to their delight, no matter how many times they replenished their vessels, the level of the wine remained exactly the same.

"'Tis true,' said Korsakov. 'That wine don't look to be getting any lower. 'Tis a miracle, lads; a gift from the Lord himself.'

The men soon spilled out onto the streets, their raucous laughter and bawdy drinking songs alerting those who had not ventured from their houses for the best part of two days.

'Why,' said one old woman in a kerchief and sheepskins. 'It be the menfolk over at Maximov's. And it looks like they've been drinking.'

'Hey, granny,' shouted Priapikov. 'Come and have a glass with us. We've taken over the place. Now there won't be any laws against good honest folk enjoyin' 'emselves.'

Eager to get something for nothing, especially the wine they had been forbidden of late, a few of the older townsfolk shuffled over to the house and partook of a glass or two.

'You're right,' said the old woman who first spotted them. 'That's right good stuff, that is.'

In high spirits, the men wanted everyone to feel as good as they did, and they swarmed all over town, returning to their homes. But most of their families had been through sleepless nights full of worry, some had lost loved ones or suffered serious injury, and the last thing they wanted to do was participate in some drunken orgy. When the men burst into their cottages or shacks, therefore, they received a far from enthusiastic welcome. And it was this indifference that sealed the town's fate.

THE HOLY DRINKER

Drunk and unreasonable, the men's joy quickly turned to anger. To be shouted at infuriated them. After shivering in both forest and prison cell, before liberating the holy wine for all to enjoy, they saw it as an ungrateful gesture. In their minds they should have been treated like heroes not villains.

As a result, arguments broke out between husbands and wives, old men and young, sons and daughters. Babies cried. Children pulled at their parents' clothes, begging them to stop shouting at each other.

In Zakharov's shack, his stout, chubby-faced wife was in no mood to put up with his mischief.

'Come on, Olga, have a sip of this wine.'

'Get away from me, you drunken fool,' she said, shoving him so hard he fell flat on his backside, banging his head against the stove. 'I'm sick of your drunken antics. Where were you when the young 'uns were crying their eyes out, eh?'

In Priapikov's cottage, his young bride, already showing signs of her first child, repelled his drunken advances.

'Get a drop of this down you, Dunya. It'll put you in the mood for a little loving.'

'Loving!' she cried, picking up a sharp knife from the table. 'I'll give you loving, if you try and lay one of your filthy hands on me.'

'What? Put that thing down, woman! I be the master of this house. And if I want what by rights of marriage I'm due, I shall take it.'

In Nazar Marka's shack, his old wife armed herself with a wooden club.

'Get yourself 'round that stove, Ivana, and roast me up some meat.'

'Roast you up some meat! You've got to be joking, you pie-eyed brute. We ain't got no meat! We never have no meat!'

And it was these fiery domestic disputes, not light-hearted revelry that now spilled out onto the streets.

The market square became a battlefield. The men with their bottles of wine continued to argue with their wives, fathers, mothers and children. Blows as well as angry words were exchanged. One after another, shop windows were smashed and stalls upturned. A fire broke out, spreading on the gusting wind, great flames rising from the

131

roofs of the shops and adjoining houses. Nobody seemed to notice or care, too busy were they arguing and fighting amongst themselves.

Doctor Rimsky ran out into the streets.

'My God!' He looked around, shaking his head. 'Look what's become of us! Stop it, damn you!'

But no matter how many times he appealed to men whose children he had brought into the world, whose ailments he had treated with such care and consideration, men who, up until that moment, had afforded him the utmost reverence, they would not listen. They pushed him aside, spat out threats and raised their hands, as if they would turn on him next. This shocked and saddened Doctor Rimsky. But what troubled him most of all was the horrible look in their drink-reddened eyes, as if they were no longer in possession of their minds.

In desperation, he ran all the way to Maximov's house, finding a dozen or so men in the old merchant's room, some crowded round the vat of wine, others passed out in puddles of their own urine or vomit.

'Ah, the good Doctor,' said Korsakov, swinging a bottle above his head. 'Come and have a glass of wine (hiccup). We won't be stingy, not like those army boys. We'll share this stuff out amongst our brothers and sisters. On that you can rest assured.'

Rimsky glared at him.

'You're drunk, man. You don't know what you're talking about.' He marched over, grabbed Korsakov under the arms, and somehow lifted the great drunken lump to his feet. 'Come into the hall.' He shuffled Korsakov out of the door. 'Look.' Out of the window black smoke could be seen billowing from the rooftops. 'Do you not see what you've done? Your wine, as you call it, has set the whole town ablaze.'

Korsakov swayed and blinked his eyes, but was incapable of taking anything in.

'Ah, don't you (hiccup) worry 'bout all that.' He said, turning back in the direction of Maximov's room. 'It'll sort itself out. Now…come you inside, Doctor. I owe you a drink after you saved my youngest boy from that cough of his. We'll raise a glass to you, and to old Maximov himself, without whom none of this would've been possible.'

Rimsky shook his head, raced down the stairs and exited the house.

When news of the disturbances reached the garrison, Belanov gathered his men outside the main barracks. Most had only just returned from the forest and looked wearied from two sleepless days and nights spent outdoors, riding over rough terrain, with barely a mouthful of wholesome food to eat.

'The situation in town has worsened considerably,' he told them. 'The menfolk have taken over Maximov's house, and gone on a drunken rampage. So we will have to proceed with utmost caution.' He pointed his riding crop at Abakumov. 'Load the heavy gun onto one of the carts. The rest of you, arm yourself with rifles and plenty of ammunition. If we enter town from the meadow, there's no reason to say we can't sneak up to Maximov's house and regain control of the property.'

The men prepared themselves like an army going into battle.

Within the hour they had assembled themselves in the meadow, spreading out along the brow of the hill, rifles poised, awaiting further instructions. Plumes of smoke still hung over the market square, and the sound of raised voices, tramping feet and smashing glass carried on the wind.

'Lieutenant,' shouted Ulitsky, rushing over. 'Doctor Rimsky is on his way up here. What shall we do?'

'The Doctor?' said Belanov. 'What on earth is he doing here?' He raised his field-glasses. 'Er, let him pass.'

Rimsky strode over the hill, marching straight up to Belanov.

'Lieutenant, I must speak with you. I–'

'How did you know of our presence, Doctor?' said Belanov, his nostrils twitching out his disproval.

'A young lad saw you from the forest,' he replied. 'When I heard, I knew I had to update you on the situation at Maximov's house.'

'You've been inside?'

'Yes, not more than an hour or so ago.'

'And what's going on in there?' asked Belanov. 'Are the men heavily-armed? Have they constructed any barricades and taken up defensive positions?'

'Far from it,' Rimsky replied. 'They're completely drunk, that's what they are. I doubt many of them could hold a rifle, let alone fire one. And that's why I wanted to speak to you. If you conduct your operation with suitable restraint, I'm sure you could march into the house without so much as firing a shot. There need not be any further bloodshed.'

Belanov let out a condescending chuckle.

'Doctor, Doctor, Doctor,' he said. 'I know you mean well, but complex military operations are hardly in your line of expertise, now, are they?'

'No, of course not,' the doctor flared up. 'But the townsfolk have suffered greatly these last few days. A massacre is the last thing they deserve.'

Belanov's nostrils twitched again.

'That goes without saying, Doctor. And your comments have been noted. Now, if you would be so kind as to return to town, I have an operation to coordinate.'

If only Belanov had taken Rimsky's advice.

When his soldiers advanced towards Maximov's house, they took none of the precautions suggested, thinking it would be no more than a simple task of overrunning a few local drunks. As a result, their movements were noisy and clumsy, alerting the townsfolk, who in turn, put the troops under immediate fire, inflicting a few unnecessary casualties.

'Return fire,' Belanov shouted, ducking for cover behind the cart. 'Return fire, I said!'

The soldiers took up defensive positions and fired relentlessly, cutting down dozens of men as they rushed across the dirt-track, carrying nothing more than pieces of wood, axes or shovels. And it was not just the fugitives from the forest who came careering over from all angles, but everyone who had sampled the wine, old men and women alike. They too carried crude weapons, shouted obscenities, and had evil, twisted looks on their faces.

The men lowered their rifles, unsure if they should continue firing or not.

'Keep firing!' screamed Belanov. 'For God's sake, men, keep firing. They'll rip us to pieces otherwise. '

Another volley of gunshots rang out, cutting down another swathe of townsfolk. But incredibly, it did not seem to affect the numbers of people streaming towards the soldiers, as those who had been hit before struggled back to their feet, disregarding their injuries, as if possessed with demonic strength. Fuelled by the holy wine, men and women with blood oozing from wounds to the head and stomach, men whose arms and legs had been partially-severed, those who should by rights have been dead, rose once again, advancing on Belanov's troops.

'Why, they're out of their minds,' he cried. 'They'll stop at nothing.'

In the bloody moments that followed, more and more shots rang out, and more and more people were struck down, their corpses piled at the sides of the road, three or four deep in places, before the troops finally managed to overwhelm them.

Infuriated, realizing his mistake and reacting with vengeful disproportion, Belanov had his men position the heavy gun right opposite Maximov's house, where the remaining insurgents had retreated, and were now taking pot-shots at the soldiers.

Rimsky, risking his life, dashed across the street.

'What are you doing?' He grabbed Belanov's arm. 'You've killed half the town. I told you these men had only a few rifles between them.'

Belanov shook himself free.

'Get away from here, Doctor!' he shouted. 'This is the field of battle not an operating theatre. Make yourself useful and attend to the wounded.'

'Wounded? I doubt there's a single man or *woman* left alive. And I will make sure the highest authority in the land is aware of your indiscriminate butchery.'

This clearly rattled Belanov.

'But you saw them yourself, Doctor. They were like madmen. What else was I supposed to do? If they'd have got any closer they could have overwhelmed us.'

The gunfire coming from the house petered out.

'They've stopped firing, sir,' a soldier shouted from the front. 'What shall we do?'

'See,' said Rimsky. 'They've run out of ammunition. If only you'd waited, none of this would've happened.'

'We can't be sure of that.' Belanov walked over to the heavy gun. 'Open fire, Abakumov. I want that house levelled to the ground.'

Before Rimsky could protest, the gun exploded into life, spraying the house with bullets, splintering wooden panels, smashing what remained of the windows, until half the frontage, the dilapidated porch and a large part of the roof had crashed to the floor.

In a matter of minutes the building had been reduced to a shell.

'Ceasefire!' shouted Belanov.

They all stood in silence, watching the smoke and dust as it slowly cleared. When it had settled, not a sound of stirring could be heard from inside the house.

'Come on, Lieutenant,' said Rimsky, rushing up the garden path. 'Let's go and see what's left in there.'

Belanov followed after him.

Both men picked their way through the decimated hallway, and made their way upstairs.

In Maximov's room, twenty or so men lay sprawled across the floor, their lifeless bodies riddled with bullet wounds. Only the blood-spattered Korsakov was still moving. Propped up against the vat, he was trying to scoop some wine into his mouth.

'It's not gone down once, no matter how much we've drunk…it's not…' he trailed off, his head lolled to the side, his eyes closed, as the last breath left his body.

'Right,' said Rimsky. 'Let's get rid of this stuff once and for all.'

With an axe and shovel found in the room, they smashed the wooden vat, splintering its sides, the wine spilling over the floor, gushing out onto the landing and down the stairs, through the opened door and into the street, like a river bursting its banks.

It went on and on, as if it was never going to stop, seeping through floorboards that started to split and break up under the pressure.

'Quickly,' said Belanov, tossing his axe aside. 'We must get downstairs. I fear the ceiling is about to collapse.'

When troops from the adjoining province marched over the hill, they saw scores of dead bodies strewn across snow stained with blood. Fires smouldered from the ashes of the market square. A few old women knelt crying before corpses of their husbands, sons and daughters, nieces, nephews or grandchildren. Others in sheepskins picked through the debris, trying to salvage something from their former lives.

A lone rider galloped over to Belanov, who had just run out of Maximov's house.

'What on earth happened here, Lieutenant? It looks like absolute carnage took place, all out war.'

'That's because it was, Captain,' he replied, wiping a handkerchief across his face. 'A war against drink and the misery and destruction it brings to working people's lives.'

Chapter Eighteen

'And what happened to them folk who took a first sip of that wine?' asked Volya. 'Did they all perish at the hands of those soldiers?'

The old man ran his tongue over his cracked lips, leaned forward and rested his elbows on the table.

'Not all of 'em, no,' he replied. 'As you probably guessed, the heathen, the drinker, Maximov, the scourge of that town, was never seen again. To this day, though, people still talk 'bout him and tell stories just like mine. But no one had ever heard of a man turning into a vat of wine before, so most just laughed it off, presuming it was some superstitious nonsense. But I tell you, lads, things happen in this life that can't be explained. And what I've just told you took place just the way I said it did. Whether you choose to believe me or not is up to you.'

We all exchanged grave looks.

'Even stranger, though,' the old man continued, 'was the fate of Marfa Orlova…'

In the aftermath of the massacre, no trace of the old woman's body was found in the shell of Maximov's house. Outraged by Belanov's excesses, Doctor Rimsky wanted every corpse accounted for so he could record an official death-toll in the letter he intended to write to the Tsar, outlining the brutal scale of the tragedy. In the morning he had soldiers search all around the yard, for he knew a woman in

138

Marfa Orlova's condition could not venture far, but still, they found nothing.

Months later, when some semblance of normality had returned, disturbing stories began to circulate. In the night, people reported seeing a vision of a frail, white-haired old woman outside the tavern, banging on the windows, shouting Maximov's name. Most thought this was Marfa Orlova's spirit, a soul not at rest, damned to spend the rest of its days between one world and the next, looking for her missing master. Never would the cursed woman be at peace until she discovered his fate.

The day after all that killing, Rimsky called round to Chernov's house. After searching every room, he found the moneylender's corpse upstairs, in a pitiful state. In all likelihood, driven out of his mind with alcoholic cravings, he had consumed bottles of cologne and raw spirit, anything with a trace of alcohol in it, and suffered the most horrible of deaths, all alone in his big empty house, with no one to comfort him or come to his aid.

From his initial examination, the doctor could tell that Chernov's liver, the biggest organ in the human body, had failed, and knew, therefore, that his last few hours had been spent in excruciating pain. For when the liver shuts down, the body is subject to all kinds of shudders and convulsions, intense stomach and chest pains, bleeding from every orifice, retching and fever.

Before he left the house, Rimsky took one last look at the body: the skin a dark ugly yellow colour, the puffy eyes, the twisted features, bloodstained shirt front, the faecal stench, and thought to himself, all this for the sake of a drink.

But perhaps Pogbregnyak's story was most bizarre of all. After a spell in prison for his attack on Marianka (which left the poor girl blind in one eye and with a permanent limp), he joined a band of religious fanatics, castrates they were, who wandered barefoot all over our vast nation, spreading their own version of the Gospel. By all accounts, Pogbregnyak did a lot of soul-searching in prison, renouncing all forms of earthly pleasure. When he looked back over his debauchery and the way he ruined so many lives, he knew he had to make a serious change. In his spare time he read the Scriptures, and came under the influence of another reformed soul, a raging syphilitic, so it transpired, who was intent on joining that band of fanatics as soon as his sentence was served.

Pogbregnyak agreed to go along with him.

The procedure itself took place in R., not a few hundred versts from this very town. One morning, Marianka received a package in the post, along with a short letter from Pogbregnyak. He did not ask for forgiveness, saying only the Lord could offer that, but wished her all the happiness in the world. To show his sincerity he had sent her his severed genitals. So rotten were they, maggots were said to be crawling out of 'em, and the stench did not leave Marianka's cottage for over a year.

The two priests, Zubov and Semyon, fared little better. No more than ten versts from town, their carriage was forced from the road by bandits; a nasty bunch with no respect for God or man. They bundled the two priests out of the carriage and searched through their belongings, stumbling upon twenty cases of red wine. Their elation could not have been greater had they discovered a chest full of gold pieces.

Unable to contain themselves, they started to drink the wine at the roadside. When the priests protested, the men dragged them and the driver into a nearby field and cut their throats. Weeks later, during the spring thaw, three bodies were found with terrible injuries, animals having ripped off half their faces and eaten their insides. One can only hope they were long dead before the foxes, rats and big birds of prey found them.

As a postscript to the priests' bloody demise, a band of armed men were said to have gone on a drunken rampage in the region, riding from village to village, killing any man who stood in their way, and raping women and young girls alike (some years away from maturity.) How and when they met their end remains unclear.

And the tragedy was not confined to the town alone. When word of Captain Levsky's death reached Petersburg, his father, the highly decorated officer, the tyrant who never once showed his son any affection, suffered a major breakdown. For days, he locked himself away in his study, barely eating, drinking, or exchanging words with his servants. Whenever they knocked on the door, he admonished them so severely they dare not try again.

Only when a single gunshot rang out did they attempt to force their way inside, finding the old man slumped over his writing desk, an antique duelling pistol in one of his hands, before him a suicide note. In the letter he outlined his grief over his only child's passing, saying he could no longer live without his beloved son, expressing his deep regret for his treatment of the boy when he was younger, and how he wished he had done so many things differently. The only reason he acted so sternly, he went on to say, was because he wanted the best for his sole heir, wanted him to grow into a strong and worthy servant of the Tsar.

Heartbreakingly, he closed the letter as follows: "the most painful thing about my son's death is that he never knew how much I loved him."

His suicide caused quite a stir in Petersburg. The bullet wound was rumoured to be so precise, not a drop of blood spilled from the old man's body.

'And what happened to young Peter?' asked Volya. 'Him who was dishing out all that free wine? Didn't he tell the doctor he was going back to his shack for something, just after his mother died? Then you never mentioned him again.'

The old man touched the bandages covering his eyes.

'Aye, you're right. That's one part of the story I left untold.'

As you probably gathered, there had been little joy in Peter's short life, with his brothers and father killed, and his poverty-stricken mother bed-bound. In many ways he looked upon Maximov as his only remaining family. And even though the old merchant treated the boy badly, he undoubtedly had a lot of affection for him. This only came out when he had had a glass or two of vodka, though. Like most drinking men, Maximov found it hard to express his feelings without a drop of alcohol inside him.

Regardless, Peter loved accompanying Maximov to the tavern, or on one of his drinking sprees. Most of all, he loved to listen to him tell stories, even if he had heard a tale countless times before, there was always something slightly different in the way Maximov told it. What fascinated Peter was the moment the old man came to the end of some unlikely yarn, how he teased his listeners along before delivering a funny or shocking punch-line, and how everyone laughed and patted him on the back. In these moments, a look of satisfaction broke out across Maximov's face, because he knew he had the power to enchant, to hold people enrapt, that he had the kind of charisma not many men are blessed with. And whenever he lost his temper, shouted at or berated Peter, he never forgot that look on his master's face, because he knew it was the mark of a special individual.

As he grew towards manhood, Peter often wondered what made Maximov like that, what changed him from a cantankerous miser to a mesmerizing storyteller, who could enthrall people from all walks of life. And of course, he came to the conclusion that it was all the wine and vodka he drank. Therefore, Maximov's warnings, telling him to never touch the stuff, that it was evil, that it ruined the health, that it prevented a man from satisfying a woman, only fired his curiosity.

After those tragic few days in town, Peter decided it was time for him to finally get drunk; to transform himself like Maximov had done so often in the past. Perhaps, deep down, the boy had always wanted to be somebody else, and when he saw what the wine had done for his mother, granting her wish of death, he reckoned it would grant him his most prized wish too: to get away from that poky little town once and for all, to travel to far-away places, to see wild and exotic things, to chase after beautiful women, to roam with all the freedom of a bird soaring the skies.

Leaving Rimsky's side, he rushed back to his shack and dug out a bottle of wine he had hidden when he first started taking it from

Maximov's vat. In the darkness, his mother's skeletal corpse in the next room, he drank it down, closed his eyes, and sure enough was transported off on a voyage of discovery.

First he saw himself on the deck of a great sailboat, racing over a glistening stretch of ocean. The sun beat down. The sea-salted wind lashed into his face, and rustled against the great sails above, powering the vessel through the water. He had never felt so alive and exhilarated, inspired and so full of possibilities. All around, as far as his eyes could see, a deep-blue vastness heaved and rippled, off into the endless horizon of a man's most fantastical imaginings.

He looked down.

Dolphins swam alongside the boat and flying fish of rainbow hues leapt through the air. He had never seen anything so spectacular, and desperately wanted to be a part of it, of nature, of all living things. Stripping off his clothes, he clambered overboard and jumped into the cool water. As it enveloped him, he swam amongst the striking, multi-coloured fish, before diving to the very depths of the ocean.

Next, Peter saw himself walking the streets of a vast and beautiful city, past elegant buildings, bronze cupolas, winding canals, embankments and bridges, teeming thoroughfares and alluring shops. It was like some magical world.

'Petersburg,' he whispered to himself.

And he kept walking and walking, fixing his eyes on all these wondrous sights, until he found himself in the Summer Gardens, amongst beautiful young women in beautiful clothes.

One girl in particular caught his eye, with her blonde curls resting at a shoulder's-length, porcelain skin, and a sweet smile playing on her full red lips.

She walked over and took hold of his hand

'Hello,' she said. 'My name's Natasha. I'm going to be your wife.'

In an instant their whole life together flashed through Peter's mind: their first kiss, all the tender intimacies he never thought someone from his background would ever experience. He walked around their house, with its palatial living and dining rooms, handcrafted furniture, crystal chandeliers, thick oriental rugs, and exquisite paintings on the walls. He sat at a fine table and ate a fine meal. He drank ruby-red wine from a long-stemmed glass. He walked up a winding staircase. In the nursery, his smiling wife handed him their first-born child.

All of this gave him an excited feeling in his stomach, when that boyhood awkwardness fades and all the promises of adult life appear on the horizon, where so many things seem just within a young man's reach.

The dream vision deepened, widened, racing across the continents.

Now Peter saw himself in a sprawling jungle, where crocodiles floated atop a murky river, squawking birds with beautiful plumage fluttered in the skies, shrieking monkeys swung from tree branch to tree branch, and elephants and giraffes strutted through the undergrowth.

Peter looked around in amazement. These were the kinds of creatures he had only heard about in Maximov's unlikely stories.

Finally, Peter saw himself ascending the face of a snow-topped mountain, icy wind whistling past his face as he pulled himself up onto a precipitous ledge. Standing and straightening, he looked out over the vast mountainous range and the brilliant white peaks, and breathed the pure, crisp air deep into his lungs.

'Ahhhhhhhhhhhhhh!' he shouted. The echo reverberated around not just the mountains, but the entire planet, as if shaking it from its axis, until the whole world, and everybody in it knew Peter Petrenko's name.

When he came round, rays of morning light streamed in through the curtainless window. The shack smelt worse than it had ever smelt before; the fetid stench of decay hanging heavy in the air. He looked at his mother's bed just as a bolt of sunlight illuminated her skeleton, making it appear as if she was lurching towards him.

'Ahhhhhhhhhhhhhh!' he cried, and shooting to his feet, he bundled his way out of the door.

By the time he emerged, the gunshots and fighting had long since ceased. He walked up to what was left of Maximov's house and saw all the bodies lying in the snow: Priapikov and Tomsky, the elder,

Alenikov, who lived just across the street, old man Markov, women who were on speaking terms with his mother–dead, all of them dead. And something inside of Peter snapped, seeing all that blood and killing, the senseless waste. In a fit of despair, he sunk to his knees, dug his filthy hands with his long fingernails into his eyes, and gouged them out of their sockets.

'Why?' cried Volya. 'Why would he do such a stupid thing?'

"Cause when he looked 'round,' said the old man, 'seeing all that death and destruction, he knew there was no way he was ever going to escape from that town. He knew he was stuck there for the rest of his days and that all those visions, those dreams of sailing the seas, of walking through grand cities, of climbing mountains and trekking through rainforests, were just fantasies, things he would never get the chance to do in real life. And the thought of that was more than he could take. If he had to set his eyes on the same things day in, day out–the dirt-track, market square, meadow and forest–he would rather be blind than be able to see, for what would he be missing out on, if everything remained exactly the same?'

No one spoke for a good few moments.

'One thing confuses me, though,' said Volya. 'How was this old Maximov's fault? If he be dead, turned into a vat of wine?'

The old man's features twisted and his voice sounded much harder than before.

"Cause men like Maximov pass on their bad habits to others, to the younger generation, they're a bad example. If he had lived a clean, God-fearing life, if he hadn't been a wretched boozer, shambling from one pot-house to the next, then young Peter would never have followed his lead.'

A few grumbles broke out from the other lads.

'Sounds like the rubbish those priests spout in church,' said Volya's brother, '–"don't do this, don't do that". I reckon a man has got to find out for himself in life, and make up his own mind, not listen to do-gooding preachers like you.'

'Yeah,' said Volya. 'And how comes you know all this, old man?'

The old man got unsteadily to his feet, using the table to support himself, and slowly untwined the bandages from his face. As each one fell to the floor, we all stared at him, and nearly all of us let out a gasp when seeing the dark, empty sockets where his eyes had once been.

WINGS OF THE OVERLORD

BOOK ONE

Morton Faulkner

KNOX ROBINSON
PUBLISHING
London & New York

PROLOGUE

SONALUMES, 2050 AC

No one can ever truly know or understand these magnificent creatures -
how could they? For the Red Tellars are the Wings of the Overlord.

Dialogues of Meshanel

Snow-clad and ice-bound, the two peaks opposite rose in ragged
splendour to pierce the egg-blue sky of dawn. Wisps of cloud gusted
and swathed about the rock formations, occasionally obscuring the
chasm far below. Scattered on narrow ledges and precipitous ridges,
thousands of drab-clothed men stood or crouched, waiting.

Wrapped in an inadequate fawn-fur cloak which freezing gusts
of air threatened to whip from him, General Foo-sep braced himself
and, his clean-shaven chin set with annoyance, looked down upon his
suffering men. His gums ached dully with the insidious cold, yellow
teeth chattering. In vain he rubbed fur-gloved hands together.

An entire toumen! Ten thousand men! And they were to take orders from an accursed civilian! He seethed, casting an embittered glare to his right, at a black-clad man of slight frame, parchment-coloured skin and ebony pebbles for eyes.

The wind slapped at this man's fur cloak and whistled over the bare out-jutting rocks nearby.

Wind-howl was deafening on the outcrop up here, yet only a step back into the shelter of the overhang no sound penetrated; and from here the entire range of the Sonalume Mountains seemed enveloped in this same eerie stillness.

"They will be along soon," said the civilian, visibly tensing as he leaned over the sloping ledge. His bear-hide boots crackled as he moved, shifting ice from the soles.

Below – a dizzying drop that had claimed too many men already – the bottom indistinct in a slithering purple haze.

Foo-sep discerned the tiny motes of black in the sky and, as the shapes approached, he was struck by their immense size. Framed by the two grey-blue peaks, the birds were coming; he had to admit, grudgingly, as predicted.

"Now!" howled the civilian.

Hoarfrost encrusted brows scowling, Foo-sep lifted his arm and signalled to his men on both sides of the wide, gaping chasm.

Soundlessly, with military precision, the "prepare" signal passed through the dispersed ranks.

Foo-sep raised his eyeglass, careful lest he touched his skin with its icy rim.

Stern-faced with the cold and, at last, a sense of purpose, his loyal soldiers were now unfurling nets and arranging stones for quick reloading of their sling-shots.

Foo-sep slowly scanned across the striated rock face.

Abruptly, the birds leapt into focus, their presence taking away his breath in cold wisps. Such an enormous wingspan! And red, O so red! He hesitated at the thought of the task ahead.

Foo-sep's momentary indecision must have been communicated to the other, or perhaps the civilian possessed even more arcane powers than those with which he was credited; "The King desires it," was all he said.

Foo-sep nodded and moved the eyeglass across to the other rock face where the remaining soldiers were trying in vain to keep warm, quivers ready, bowstrings taut and poised.

Now the birds were entering between the peaks.

Foo-sep signed to a Signaller who blew three great blasts on his horn. The sound echoed among the peaks.

In a constant flurry, ice-coated nets looped out, entwining many of the creatures' wings. Some nets were sent soaring attached to arrows. Other birds swooped beneath the heavy mesh then swerved, talons raking the men responsible. Another used its wings to sweep soldiers from the ledges as though dusting furniture. Stones hit a few on their bright red crests and they plummeted, stunned, to be caught by outstretched nets beneath; nets that were slowly filling up, straining at their supports.

Watching through his eyeglass, Foo-sep was amazed at the weird silence of the birds: only their frenetically beating wings generated any sound; all other noise originated from his yelling and shrieking soldiers as they flung nets and stones or were dragged from precarious positions. He scowled as a group of fools forgot to keep clear of their own nets; entangled, they were wrenched to giddy, plunging deaths.

Pacing from side to side, Foo-sep watched helplessly as his beloved toumen was decimated. And for what? A few hundred birds!

His attention was diverted to an uncannily large specimen ensnared in nets, its feathers flying as it clawed at two soldiers on a ledge while they loosed sling-stones at the creature.

Yet the missiles had no effect, and the massive curved beak snapped through the brittle mesh as though it was flimsy plains-grass.

As the bird looped, Foo-sep noticed a distinctive marking none of the others seemed to possess – a white patch on its throat.

The civilian must have observed it also, because at that instant he gripped Foo-sep's arm, lips visibly trembling, black pebble-eyes shining. Then, in desperation, the idiot shouted an order that made no sense at all: "Let that one go!"

Numb with cold, bitterly aware of how many good men had suffered already at the talons of that gigantic bird, Foo-sep steeled himself against his better instinct and cupped gloved hands round his mouth.

"Let that one go!" he called.

And the words echoed, mocking: *"Let that one go!"*

PART ONE
THIRD SAPIN - FOURTH SABIN OF JUVOUS

The Song of the Overlord – Part the First:
How to explain the omniscient Overlord?
How shall I define what thing He is?
Chance is a word without reason;
Nothing can exist without a cause.
So it is with Him –
Wholly existent, and yet non-existent.
Whatever becometh naught out of entity
The meaning of that nothingness is He.

CHAPTER ONE

QUEST

It is an unknown quantity veiled in a mystery within an enigma.
The Book of Concealed Mystery (Ascribed to Lhoretsorel)

After-morning sunlight streamed through the high windows to illuminate the Long Gymnasium and its polished wooden walls which were festooned with all kinds of physical training apparatus. The floor was a series of padded rush mats. The huge room dwarfed the seven people here.

The tension was almost palpable to the two onlookers as four prospective employees of the Red Tellar Inn advanced soundlessly, their eyes flashing warily at Ulran, the innman.

Behind Ulran, his son Ranell stood by the tall ironwood doors with Ulran's aide, the short black-skinned Aeleg.

Of the four enlistees, only Yorda and Krailek on the left gave the impression of being at ease; their movements were measured, eyes never leaving Ulran's.

Enlistment combat was traditionally unarmed and this day's would not deviate from the norm, though for reasons of honour no contender was ever searched. While these four wore their own colourful street clothes – breeches, boots and jerkins – Ulran, in complete contrast, stood barefoot, garbed in a single long voluminous garment of jet black, his left breast emblazoned with an embroidered white sekor.

Ulran's wide brown eyes studied the approach of the combatants.

Meetel was dark, tall and powerfully built. His long black hair streamed behind him as he rushed first, shrieking defiance. He had nerve – but no technique. With little effort Ulran skipped to safety. Close on Meetel's heels came Ephanel and the other two. Ulran ducked and weaved out of reach of grasping hands, flailing feet and fists.

By now all four must have realised there were no openings in the garment Ulran wore: he used neither arms nor legs to block or counter-attack: his speed was sufficient to avoid contact. They circled Ulran in a wary, predatory fashion.

As Meetel charged with rigid fingers lancing at the innman's eyes, Ulran lowered his head of straight short black hair and Meetel's fingers shattered on impact with cranium-bone. Ulran swiftly moved away, leaving Meetel on one knee, tears of pain streaming as he clutched a broken hand.

Ephanel was squat and too muscular. His sallow features twisted as he delivered a tremendous kick.

Robes cracking with the sudden movement, the innman leapt high above the out-thrust leather boot and, as though from nowhere, the innman's legs whipped out from the material, full into Ephanel's stomach. The kick's force hurled Ephanel head over heels to land noisily among weights and dumb-bells. Ephanel was completely taken by surprise.

Without any openings save that for the wearer's head and feet, the garment's special properties were impressive. With the right force and inclination, the cloth could be penetrated easily and when the limb was again withdrawn into the folds, the opening would seal, leaving no trace. But if the right force could not be mastered, then the garment was little better than a burial shroud.

Krailek was short and wiry, his face careworn by weather and travel; his blue eyes darted to left and right, gauging distances. Yorda was tall with well-toned muscles, and deceptively light on his feet. Both, obviously determined on a joint action, simultaneously attacked Ulran from each side.

Ulran leapt in front of Krailek on his left, arms suddenly shooting out of the black garment; the surprise had hardly left Krailek's lined, weather-beaten face when he found himself grabbed, stunned and swinging in an arc towards the astonished Yorda. Both tumbled into the nearby wall, dazed and bruised.

Turning, Ulran reflected his son Ranell's fleeting smile: two would prove suitable for probationary employment. Yorda and Krailek. They would require a great deal of training to be a match for the rest of his men, but they had that special intelligent spark that –

Only one lightning-fast blow was necessary, delivered as Ulran pivoted on buckling knees: the punch, angled upwards, thudded into Meetel's solar plexus and seemed to travel through bone and flesh, rupturing the man's heart.

A small dagger fell from lifeless fingers and Ulran grasped it before the handle hit the floor.

A nasty weapon with serrated edges pointing to the hilt, it would extract entrails, flesh and muscle on withdrawal from the wound. Ulran knew it well: a tukluk, the brainchild of the Brethren of the Sword, the Gild of the Mercenaries. Ulran shook his head. "A man who would savour another's pain or misery," he mused, turning to the slowly recovering participants. "The test is not to win but to see how the fight is fought – and, indeed, how it is lost."

Without another word, he strode from the Long Gymnasium with his son and his aide close behind.

Established in 1480AC on the occasion of the First Festival of Brilansor, the Red Tellar Inn was situated in Marron Square in the Three Cities that comprised Lornwater.

People from all the outlying cities knew of the renowned Red Tellar, for in all Floreskand it was the only inn equipped with duelling rooms. Its ten-storey height alone would draw attention, twice as high as any other known inn, and only overshadowed in Lornwater by the two Minars and the Eyrie above the Old City's Palace.

There were many specialised chambers, among them music and shrine rooms, hotel rooms, Staff residences, private duelling rooms, the beer-hall and the Long Gymnasium.

Both wings of the building consisted of three floors: looking down from his tenth storey office, Ulran gazed upon the vast variety of colour blossoming in the roof garden.

Decorative shagunblend lamps tinted sunlight in his office. Ulran divested himself of the Jhet-fibre garb and slowly his thick lips curved in a sanguinary grin. He pictured again the disconcerted look on Meetel's face.

Perhaps then, at the instant on the Edge – the moment between life and death – Meetel had comprehended that the cloth was the fabled Jhet-fibre woven by Seamstresses from the Fane of the Overlord itself.

Ulran washed then dried himself on a small towel and donned a silk shirt from the wardrobe and a pair of loose-fitting cotton trousers which he tucked into brown hide boots.

In a rare moment of reverie, he idly fingered the large wall-chart that reminded him of the travels he and Ranell had made.

Ranell was quick to learn; yet after all his training he still possessed a stubborn streak. Still, he'd done well, considering he had lacked a mother's warmth and love almost since birth. Ulran felt he could be justly proud of his son as the youth approached full adulthood.

A distinctive knock sliced into his thoughts.

"Come in, Ranell."

Though shorter than his sire, Ranell was otherwise in every way Ulran's progeny, from his dark wavy hair, glistening alert brown eyes and almost classical facial features, to his slim yet powerfully muscled physique. He stood in the doorway that led into the anteroom; there, Ranell performed the duties of secretary to his father, in preparation for the day when he would succeed him to become Innman, Red Tellar.

Formally, he gave a respectful nod. "Begetter," he said, assuming the common family address for an esteemed father. "There's a strange silent fellow in the passage waiting to see you." His eyes gleamed, amused. "He speaks with an air of the arcane about him and is weighted down with countless talismen."

"And what did you say?"

"I expressed sincere apologies for having kept him waiting and requested that he be patient while I ascertained when or if you would be available..."

"But didn't you ask him his business here?"

"Yes, Begetter – I tried, but he just smiled knowingly and said his business was with you."

"I see."

"He's unarmed – and looks as though he wouldn't know which end of a sword to hold were he given one!"

"Very good. I'll see this mysterious visitor now."

At that moment Aeleg stepped in, his old skin creased in anxiety. "Ulran!" he said, breathless. "Thousands of them! Sky's full!" His thyroidal eyes shone in excitement. "Never so many before – Red Tellars!"

Scalrin. Heart hammering though outwardly calm, Ulran brushed past his son and aide and, ignoring the seated stranger, he leapt the stairs three at a time to the roof.

The midday sky was brimful with Red Tellars. The entire populace of Lornwater seemed to be out – on the street, rooftops, city walls or at windows – looking at these mystical creatures.

Even Ulran's height was dwarfed by the bird's wingspan. With bristling carmine red feathers, yellow irises and darting black slit-pupils, the Red Tellar appeared a formidable bird, predatory in mien, an aspect completed with lethal talons and huge curved beak. And yet not one living soul, Ulran included, had once reported seeing a Red Tellar eat. To compound the enigma surrounding them, they were rarely observed landing anywhere. And apart from the muted whisper of their wings, they created no sound at all – unlike the local avians that infested most eaves, lofts and trees in the city.

Ulran burst out onto the inn's flat roof as a shadow darkened the area.

A solitary Red Tellar broke formation and dived down from the main body. Ulran instinctively glanced back at Aeleg and Ranell;

but Scalrin's sharp eyes had spotted them and he veered over to the opposite side of the roof.

A slight crack of mighty wings, then the bird was down, talons gripping the low wall by a shrine to Opasor, lesslord of birds.

Ulran motioned for the others to stay where they were.

Aeleg and Ranell stared, thunderstruck that a Red Tellar should land on their roof – indeed they were nonplussed by the fact that the bird should be seen landing at all. Ulran seemed to accept this without concern.

Recognition flickered in Scalrin's eyes as Ulran knelt before the bird's great feathered chest. Without hesitation the innman reached out, gently stroked the upper ridge of the bird's beak and smoothed the silken soft crest.

In answer, Scalrin's ear feathers ruffled and he settled, pulling his greater wing coverts well into his body.

The innman exhaled through his nose, then relaxed, steadying his breathing till it was shallow. Ulran closed his eyes and slowly outstretched his hand again, palm flat upon Scalrin's breast. A rapid heartbeat pulsed under his palpating hand and transmitted sympathetic vibrations through his own frame.

Their rapport created a bridge and across this span came primitive communication, sense-impressions. Ulran gathered that something was seriously amiss in Arion.

Something terrible, something concerning Scalrin.

Ulran opened his eyes, surprised to discover moisture brimmed his lids for the first time since his wife Ellorn's demise.

Then Scalrin was gone, powerful primaries lifting him up to the vast multitude of his brethren. As far as the horizon they still flocked.

But what did it portend?

"Trouble in Arion?" the stranger enquired as Ulran stepped from the stairs into the passage.

Ulran did not show the surprise he felt at this disclosure.

The wiry stranger was evidently chagrined at the innman's negative response but, poise quickly regained, explained, "I walk with Osasor." An offered hand.

Ulran's enfolded it completely: a soft, yielding handshake. Not the usual type who would follow the white lord of fire, the innman thought.

"Cobrora Fhord," the stranger made the introduction, dressed sombrely in a grey cloak, charcoal tunic and trousers, colourless face angular and thin. "I can enlighten you a little on the behaviour of the Red Tellars. And I would like to join you on your journey to Arion."

Ranell appraised the stranger with quickened interest; Aeleg stared at Cobrora shrewdly.

Ulran, unblinking, said, "But I haven't mentioned that I'd go – though I was considering it."

Cobrora nervously stroked long lank black hair. Ulran noticed the glint of some kind of amulet beneath Cobrora's grey cloak. Brown eyes suddenly evasive, Cobrora Fhord murmured, "My – er, properties might prove useful – should you decide to go."

In preference, Ulran always travelled alone, in this way being responsible for himself and nobody else. But, this Cobrora – the Roumers plied the routes complete with staging posts regularly and swiftly, unmolested by villains and Devastator hordes, but even they could not have carried news of Arion's dire affairs in such a short time. And, as conclusive proof of this psychic's ability, he knew of Ulran's intentions to travel to Arion. It was just possible that the strange powers of Cobrora's spirit-lord could be of some use on the long trek to Arion.

"All right," said Ulran decisively. "But first we must arrange equipment." And, looking at Cobrora's thin city clothes, he added, "We must dress you properly for the long journey ahead. It may be summer – but the nights are harsh and the mountains will prove inhospitable."

"I have no intention of using the accredited tracks or the Dhur Bridge across Saloar Teen," Ulran said. "We'll leave by the Dunsaron Gate, stay overnight at The Inn, then head for Soemoff – about five days from Lornwater." Ulran's thick index finger traced the parchment map; an impressive red ruby sparkled on a gold ring. "Then we'll leave the

Cobalt Trail, crossing Saloar Teen at its narrowest point, the shallows – here..."

"But that way you miss the Goldalese road –"

"I don't want to go in by the front door. As you know, Arion is sealed off from all save a few necessary merchants. So, instead, we'll try getting into Arion over the Sonalumes. It'll take at least eighty days."

Cobrora's head shook. "You – we've only got seventy."

Ulran arched an eyebrow.

"I – I don't know the how or the why, but the Red Tellars are involved in some rite... which is to take place on the First Durinma of Lamous – seventy days hence."

Rolling up the map, Ulran grinned. "Then we've no time to lose – even if we shorten our journey by way of Astrey Caron Pass."

Cobrora blanched at that prospect.

Sturdier boots and tougher cloak and clothes were borrowed from the Red Tellar's ample stocks for Cobrora's use. Ulran loaned Cobrora a light sword and dirk, though one look at the city-dweller's face confirmed Ranell's first observation that Cobrora would have little inclination to use either even if life depended upon it.

Their transportation was obtained from the stables attached to the rear courtyard of the inn. "I'm afraid we've got little spare at the moment, save Sarolee, this palfrey," Ulran said, nodding at a roan the ostler was holding.

"I'm not proud," smiled Cobrora and hesitantly stroked the horse's muzzle.

Ulran's horse, Versayr, was a beautiful black stallion. Ulran also selected a pack-mule for carrying provisions: "We'll hire another mule and purchase most of our stores at Soemoff. I have no wish to alert anyone to the length of my absence."

As shadows lengthened with the approach of dusk, Ulran embraced his son in the courtyard entrance. Solemnly, the young man said, "No harm shall come to the Red Tellar, Begetter." "I know." The sureness of Ulran's tone impressed Cobrora. "Now, we'll be on our way." Marron Square, named after the great battle of Marron Marsh in 1227, was bustling with people raising banners across the streets. The two travellers shook hands with Ranell, and mounted their horses. A gentle nudge and they set off across the square, Cobrora holding onto the pack-mule's reins. Neither looked back.

Cobrora scratched an irritating itch, unaccustomed to this heavier clothing. A faint hammering of trepidation churned within, which must be controlled. A city-dweller since birth, Cobrora, apart from an occasional picnic with the gild outside the high outer city walls, had not ventured further. In fact, many people never set foot beyond the square launmark of their city-sector. Now, Cobrora couldn't really blame them.

But it was surely too late to turn back. O, by the gods, what a capricious gift this Sight was!

They cantered along the Long Causeway, the only road that ran straight through the Three Cities.

From the Red Tellar Inn to the Dunsaron Gate was a good ten launmarks; Ulran intended to get out of the city before the gates closed at sunset.

For many weeks the gossip had revolved around the forthcoming Carnival. And now Cobrora snatched snippets of dialogue from passers-by:

"Let his liver stew, I say!"

"I hear the Harladawn Players have some satirical comments on our magnanimous monarch!"

"Only yesterday a friend told me Saurosen's been hiring spies to report on our preparations and progress..."

"Typically underhand!"

"He'll ban sex next!"

"If you were wed to my husband, you'd wish he would!"

Even in adversity, some people retained a sense of humour. Perhaps it was the city's unease that affected Cobrora. Something other than the normal had drawn the city-dweller to accompany the innman.

Drawn was the right word. And to speak to Ulran like that at their first meeting! As though possessed, Cobrora thought, forthright and ironical, so unlike my true, docile self! Drawn, indeed.

"Three years since Saurosen replaced Kcarran II – three hundred it feels like!"

"Aye, he may be the fourth Saurosen, but if the Three Cities have their way, he'll be the last!"

"Hush, Lorg, that's seditious talk!"

Some mansions shone red in the sinking sun's rays, as though on fire; other adjacent dwellings were little more than timber-shacks and voluminous tents.

Many of the sidestreets carried on as normal, their entire length covered with awnings, the stalls vying for custom. Cobrora always thought they most resembled an underground city. Unpleasant smells suggested that the drainage system was not coping with the increased numbers.

A glance down adjoining thoroughfares revealed buildings on either side leaning inwards, conveying a claustrophobic atmosphere, deepening the shadows, greatly welcome in the summer heat though to be avoided at night.

Shouting from the left drew their attention.

Miners, still grimed with coal-dust, were leaving the Pick and Shovel Inn, a musty earthy place where they habitually congregated after work or before their next shift. Lornwater was built over many disused mines; now, mining continued in the suburbs, beyond the cultivated fields. Opposite this inn was a competitor, The Open House, one of ten so named and owned by Ulran's biggest rivals, a combine.

"Next shift's due back from the death-caves, soon, lads – let's meet them, toast their good health!"

"Health? Till the Carnival, anyway, then we'll see who's left alive, let alone healthy!"

"Oh, be quiet, Moaner. We'll tell him what to do with his infernal Edict!"

"Aye!" chorused the dusty-throated men.

Pausing at the Old Drawbridge, which had not been raised since the New City was built, Ulran twisted in his high tooled saddle, and waited for Cobrora Fhord to draw alongside.

"I'd say they're near the brink of rebellion," Cobrora observed.

"They'll have their Carnival, regardless of any stupid Royal Edict."

They crossed over the very old stagnant and evil-smelling moat that completely surrounded the Second and Old Cities, and passed into the Second City.

Saurosen IV had persistently deprived his people of their little pleasures; and now he had banned their annual Carnival. Considering these festivities had taken place without fail annually for 1062 years, commemorating the crowning of Lornwater's first King, Kcarran, Cobrora thought the people had taken the Edict commendably well. But, as Ulran said, they intended having their Carnival anyway!

On either side, the flat rooftops of varying heights presented a colourful display of roof-gardens and tents.

Because a large cart had lost a wheel on the Causeway and a huge crowd gathered to relieve the conveyance of its spilt merchandise, Ulran urged Versayr down a side street on a twisting turning detour over resounding cobbles amidst streets of washing and stalls.

It was a lengthy detour and Ulran didn't spare the horses or Cobrora. To their right towered the Doltra Complex – home of the wealthy – perched upon huge stone-block pylons and looking obscenely bright and clean in comparison with the dark and sullied earth surrounds beneath it. Nobody walked near the Doltra Complex foundations, for here was situated the caved-in remains of an older city, which had collapsed in 1823; city and King Kculicide had perished, falling into flooded mines and into the dread hands of the Underpeople.

The Second City, thought Cobrora with irony, evinced a conspicuous change. Markedly fewer preparations for the Carnival ensued here; the inhabitants were more reserved and few freely expressed opinion on the monarch and his infamous Edict.

As speedily as possible through winding streets, they returned to the Causeway.

At the tall Old City gates, Ulran reined in.

The slave market was evidently closing; the bartering and ogling crowds had dispersed, apparently uninspired by the remaining merchandise: a willowy youth and a pregnant middle-aged woman.

Ulran hailed the Slaver: "You!"

Head jerking up, the Slaver grinned with a toothless mouth, "Me, Sir?" He fingered his flamboyant tunic then, his sixth sense seeming to apprise him of a potential sale, his hands rubbed oilily together. "You want to buy the boy, my Lord?"

Ulran shook his head. "The woman – how much?"

"But she can't do much work – not far off term, I reckon... Now, the boy, he may be slender – but a little work'd soon build his muscles. Why not –?"

"The woman, Slaver." Ulran withdrew the purse from his belt, unfastened its strings. "How much?"

The Slaver's face contorted in thought, then: "Shall we say two sphands?"

"You can say what you like, but I'm offering fourteen carsts – take it or leave it. No-one else will buy her – two mouths to feed and incapable of working for her or her brat's keep."

Sighing resignedly, the Slaver nodded. "As you say, my Lord."

Ulran handed down a small gold sphand and four silver coins. "When you've closed down for the night, take the woman to the Red Tellar. Say Ulran sent her. My son Ranell will make the arrangements."

At mention of the inn and the innman's name, the Slaver's artful eyes widened and he nodded repeatedly. "Yes, sir, yes, I'll do as you bid – straight away. You'll not regret doing business with me, sir." Taking up the hastily scrawled bill-of-sale, Ulran beckoned the gravid woman.

Waddling a little with the weight of child, she stood before him in bare feet and, head held high, her eyes levelled on his, pupils glinting red in the waning sun.

"When you enter the Red Tellar," he said, "you're a free woman. Ranell, my son, will care for you in labour and after." Shock showed but briefly in her deep brown eyes. There was unquestioning acceptance in her curt nod and she backed away. Ulran turned to Cobrora who had watched the whole transaction with avid curiosity. "Come, Cobrora, let us move on. It will soon be dark."

Directly opposite the slave market stood one of many city fanes. Built of gold in the form of a pyramid, the Fane of Jahdemore, Great-Lord of day, burned in the vermilion sunlight of day's-end.

Upon a plinth at the head of the wide shallow entrance steps sat the imposing statue of the great Meshanel, Jahdemor's prophet, his sightless eyes seemingly omniscient, a trick of light. Even at this early juncture in the Carnival's arrangements, the fane pillars, doorways and arches were garlanded with sweet-scented crimson sekors, the flowers of the Light-bringer.

Blending with the shadows cast by the entrance columns stood two robed men whose intentions clearly had nothing to do with the worship of the god of light and strength, though the exquisite garb of one blatantly indicated that he was rich enough to do so.

Rashen Pellore wore rather tattered dun-coloured clothes and old sandals and silently cursed his companion for drawing attention to them. He had no difficulty recognising Badol Melomar beneath the thin disguise of false goatee, moustache and shadowy cloak-hood. The ruthless head and innman of the powerful Open House Combine was too distinguishable because of his singular ugliness to go unnoticed, Rashen thought unkindly, inwardly chuckling.

By the gods, Badol was simple! Yet, Rashen warned himself, this innman was also very rich and powerful: and, more dangerous still, he was incredibly greedy. No, he didn't really have to be a Mercenary of long standing to guess why Badol had approached him: the vendetta between the Open House Combine and the Red Tellar was no secret.

"Can I count on you, then?" Badol asked, peering at the Mercenary down the length of his sharp nose. "To deal once and for all with that upstart?" And, thick lips upturned in an unprepossessing scowl, he gestured with distaste towards the horseback figure bargaining with the sycophantic Slaver.

Pointedly ignoring Badol, Rashen silently appraised Ulran's powerful frame and effortless manner: not a movement wasted, wholly at ease. This was the first time he had seen the illustrious innman. He could see no talisman whatsoever dangling from the innman's person or horse. Obviously a man in complete harmony with the gods, an enviable state of mind indeed, he mused, fingering his own snakeskin necklace.

Rashen grinned. So unlike Ulran's companion, though! From both sides of Cobrora's palfrey and also from the tunic and belt, all manner of potion-pouches and talismen dangled and chinked.

"As you well know, the Kcarran Carnival pulls all sorts of people from all over the country," Rashen remarked icily, still studying Ulran. "There'll be plenty of opportunists and fellow-Mercenaries employed as bodyguards for the rich and fat travellers. Don't worry, I'll have my men hand-picked by sunset and we'll be on their trail at dawn."

Snatching a glimpse of Badol's moist lips forming a protest, he added, "Soon enough... I mean, you wouldn't want the foul deed committed on your own threshold, would you?"

Badol paled, shook his head vigorously.

"I thought not," said Rashen.

The Open House innman wrapped his resplendent cloak tightly about him and shakily proffered a small leather pouch; its contents jingled. "As agreed, then – half now, the rest when you bring me Ulran's ruby ring of the Red Tellar?"

Weighing the pouch thoughtfully, Rashen smiled darkly. He absently brushed his drab brown cloak. "What's to stop me teaming up with Ulran and taking his ring with his permission, just to fool you and get your money?"

Badol's lower lip trembled, saliva dribbled, and his brows knitted together. "You – you couldn't – I know Ulran. Nothing short of death would part him from that ring."

"For some men, even death has no power over them; remember that," snapped Rashen, ill-at-ease with his contract of hire. Sometimes, he wondered why his blood flowed in the way of a Mercenary. Abruptly, Rashen turned on his heel, threadbare cloak swirling, and flung over his shoulder, "I'll be back within eight days... then you'll be able to take over the Red Tellar, lock, stock and barrel, Badol Melomar!"

The innman convulsed with a tremor of fear and stared coldly after the laughing Mercenary who tossed and caught the purse of gold as though it were a mere plaything.

That morning's shaky resolve was now firm: the Mercenary and his brood, whoever they might be, must be eliminated once the death of Ulran was assured. Mercenaries and creatures of their ilk knew no loyalty to employers, he was sure. No, he couldn't risk them living, no, not at any price!

Stroking the itching false beard and moustache, Badol Melomar glared at Ulran and his incongruous companion as they passed through the Old City gates. But his countenance softened as he pictured the vast revenues of the Red Tellar at last within his grasp.

"Why, Cobrora?" Ulran repeated as they rode to the Main Plaza, the largest square in Lornwater. "Let us just say I had a feeling of kinship with that unborn babe."

Unlike the two outer cities, the Old City was formed on a strict grid plan. Here, there were no outward signs of the forthcoming Carnival. The tall buildings of the Palace would have something to do with that, thought Cobrora.

It was always the rich who stuck with Saurosen IV; and the rich lived in their mansions, here in the Old City or protectively closeted themselves in the Doltra Complex, cocooned, looking out at the world through the pretty smaltglass windows. But they didn't see the real world, Cobrora realised, surprised at such thoughts. Ulran's gesture with that slave woman had had quite an effect.

They rode past numerous fanes festooned with the appropriate sekors of their gods. The brothels on each side of the square were prospering, eagerly making welcome the many newcomers to the city.

The lowing of cattle and the stench of the livestock's excrement engulfed them. A cattle market was still embroiled in the business of auctioning. Torches were lit to combat the deepening dusk, naked flames flashing in the frightened beasts' eyes and upon their huge curved horns.

Once at Dunsaron Gate, they had to pull their mounts to one side to make way for three loaded wagons bringing in the old shift of miners.

The eyes of both male and female miners glared white and forlorn, bizarre sad contrasts to the theatrical black faces and pink mouths. Exhaustion was etched around their eyes and in the stoop of shoulders, bodies now permanently misshaped. They worked for a pittance and had little to look forward to, save their Carnival which celebrated a good and memorable king's reign. And now the worst king in recent history decreed there would be no more play, only work and more work.

Cobrora suddenly felt all apprehensions disappear as they rode through the last city gate. To get away was like clearing the mind after a heady bout of mindsaur smoking.

The road straight on led to the mines, but Ulran took another, less used track.

Almost everyone kept clear of this road.

Fresh disquiet assailed Cobrora, clutching a talisman, then another, strangling each evil effigy in turn; then whispering a succinct prayer to the most sacred gods for protection, for they were heading towards The Inn.

Feeling at odds, Cobrora looked back at the exceedingly high outer grey-stone walls of the vast city of Lornwater.

Home, with its defensive towers, its sinister crenellations spreading as far as the eye could see; the Palace Minars, the dominating Eyrie, all now bathed in silver moonlight. The moon was approaching its last Quarter, its surface without blemish or crater, intensely bright, transforming the land into an eerie ghostlike place.

Cobrora had never been outside the city when the gates were shut; now the sound carried, of the ponderous bolts thudding home.

Loneliness fell with complete suddenness.

Cobrora eyed the warm orange halo arching above the Three Cities' forbidding silhouette. A distinctive thin streamer of blue-grey smoke issued from the smalthouse and joined the many other smoke-trails of the great city.

Turning to look upon the vast night-sky, Cobrora shuddered involuntarily, wondering at the absurd relief felt on leaving the city a short while ago.

The road was a little uneven in places where the recent rains had collected. On either side crouched shapeless bushes of muskflower: threatening, sinister. The stridulation of night-devils sent Cobrora's spine tingling uncomfortably.

Presently, the road curved gently downwards, to the shore of Lornwater Lake.

"The Lake", whispered Cobrora, unable to repress a shudder.

The roan's ears pricked and the animal shied.

The evil waters – where to drink even a drop meant hideous death.

Clasping talismen tightly, prayers tumbling from trembling lips, Cobrora looked down and across the expanse of still, dark water and noticed with unease that the surface bore no reflection, neither of the stars nor of the moon. No silvery ripples like the city ponds at night. No mirror-image of the window-lit Lornwater Inn by its shores.

Cold clammy panic swelled up into Cobrora's throat, hands tensed to jerk on the reins. Cobrora wanted to halt, to yell for Ulran to stop, unwilling to have anything to do with either Lake or Inn. Yet, no sound came out and Sarolee tentatively cantered forward.

"We'll spend tonight here," Ulran said, dismounting in front of Lornwater Inn.

Lightning Source UK Ltd.
Milton Keynes UK
UKOW03n1558050614

232913UK00001B/1/P